Shame

Marged Lloyd Jones

gomer

First impression—2004

ISBN 1 84323 279 0

© Marged Lloyd Jones, 2004

Marged Lloyd Jones has asserted her right under the
Copyright, Designs and Patents Act, 1988, to be identified
as Author of this Work.

This book is published with the financial support of the
Welsh Books Council.

Printed in Wales at
Gomer Press, Llandysul, Ceredigion SA44 4QL

To
Myfanwy
and in memory of
Mair

Preface

I have lived to see the twenty-first century. I am an old woman, and my main interests are watching television, reading and keeping an eye on my work force. Occasionally I meditate and look back objectively on my past. I tend not to trust people, men especially. I cannot, not even today, bear a man to touch me. Why?

I had a difficult childhood – unwanted, unloved and lonely. I learnt to be satisfied with very little – not many pleasures, and even less in the way of love. I had to bear more sorrow than any child should have had to suffer. I feel very sad and even ashamed when I think back on my childhood.

1

Jini! A ridiculous name – a name given as a rule to a pet lamb or a toy poodle; and my name! And to crown it all, Jini John. I hated my name.

> Jini John is a beauty
> Jini John is so pretty
> But indeed it is a pity
> She's stuck up, and rather snooty.

That silly rhyme followed me throughout my schooldays; and it annoyed me dreadfully. But my real name, my Christian name is Mary Anne Jane – Mary after my mother's bosom friend, Anne after my paternal grandmother who lived in Pembrokeshire, and Jane after my maternal grandmother whom I never saw. She died before I was born.

But my mother has a beautiful name, an old Welsh name – Myfanwy. But my father called her Fan, a name usually given to a collie bitch, and he expected the same obedience from her, as the shepherd expected from his dog. When in a vile mood, and that was often, he would address her scornfully as *Miss* Myfanwy with the emphasis on the Miss. He was a man of many moods, fickle and changeable. Sometimes he would hug me excitedly, another time he would push me aside, and rant and swear like a madman. But it was my mother who bore the brunt of his wild behaviour. My very first memory is of my father shouting and cursing, and my mother weeping silently, burying her face in her apron.

My father was apparently determined that I should address him as Dyta, and mother as Mamo:

'Pa-pa and Ma-ma indeed – the language of the *crachach*, the bloody toffs, and if Dyta and Mamo were good enough for me, they are good enough for my child too. To hell with Pa-pa and Ma-ma.'

So I had to call my parents Dyta and Mamo, much against my mother's wishes.

We lived in a tiny white-washed cottage on the banks of a stream, and the constant murmur of water was a musical background to our living and sleeping, day and night. A peaceful sound, unless there was a storm, followed by floods, when Dyta and Mamo would carry sandbags to stop the water from flooding the house. The storms and the rushing water were frightening, and I would quietly climb up to the loft, squat in my bed and ask Jesus Christ to abate the storm and the floods. More often than not He would listen to me too.

The name of our house was Llety'r Wennol –

Swallow's Rest, and every spring the swallows would build their nests under the eaves, and twitter their chorus all day long. But if Dyta happened to be in a bad mood, he would take the cane brush and shatter their nests.

'Stinking buggers, shitting all over the walls,' would be his excuse for doing so. Mamo would gaze silently at the disaster, but I would scream, throw a tantrum, and run to hide. But the swallows learnt their lesson, and the following year they nestled out of sight at the back of the cottage. By the time Dyta had found their nests, the babies were ready to fly.

We lived in an isolated place, a dead end, but fortunately there was another cottage lower down on the banks of the stream. It was called Glan-dŵr, because of its proximity to the water. Two dear old spinsters lived there – Sara and Mari. They used to give me bread-and-butter plastered with soft brown sugar to eat, and that sugar was rationed, owing to the Kaiser's war. They were the owners of three speckled hens, and a magnificent red cockerel, which strutted around proclaiming that he was master of all he surveyed. I was afraid of the cockerel. He reminded me of Dyta. He too had red hair.

But for Sara and Mari, I would have been so lonely. It was Sara who taught me to catch sticklebacks in the stream, and to catch trout by tickling their bellies. Mamo forbade me from paddling 'in case you catch a cold, or maybe something worse.' I never did understand what she meant by 'something worse'. On fine days Sara used to greet me joyfully with the words, 'Take off your boots and stockings. We are going to mess about in the river.' They never called it the 'stream', always the 'river'. The 'messing around' meant racing paper boats, and Mari who used to watch us, and urge us on, always had a supply of home-made candies to reward the champion.

Sara and Mari never argued, never bickered. They were satisfied and contented with their lot, and their way of life. Their house appeared even poorer than ours, but they were forever cracking jokes, laughing or humming tunes. Their livestock, the red cockerel named Samson, and the three hens – Annie, Fanny and Daisy ruled their lives. The hens rarely laid eggs: 'they are too old to lay eggs' was Sara's excuse for their infertility – but that was not sufficient reason to do away with them.

Our cottage was tiny, just the kitchen, the end room, and the cockloft, with a ladder leading to it, where I slept. There was also a zinc shed attached to the house, where Mamo used to scrub and wash clothes, wash the dishes, and perform every dirty chore. In that same shed, I would have my bath in a zinc tub every Saturday night, summer and winter.

Mamo would attempt to cook on the open fire in the kitchen. The only utensils available were a large cast-iron kettle to heat the water, a boiler for cooking *cawl* and meat, and a large frying pan – all perched on a tripod, over a log fire. All cooking had to be confined to suit the utensils, and the food often reeked of wood smoke.

Dyta continually complained of Mamo's cooking – 'You're bloody hopeless' he used to say. But sometimes, very infrequently, he would kiss her lightly on the cheek and say, 'Bloody great, Fan'. She would then blush, and everybody would be happy – happy just for a few minutes.

Dyta was a dissatisfied man, always grumbling, always shouting, always cursing and ranting. It was Mamo who was blamed for every little thing. I hated it, and I used to run down to Glan-dŵr to escape from the rumpus and the quarrelling. Sara and Mari would pamper and embrace me. Sara especially.

She would hug and cuddle me, and the old rocking chair would groan to the rhythm of her soothing tune.

> Jini is my darling
> My darling, my darling
> Jini is my darling
> So sweet and always smiling.

They never questioned me about life at home; never asked me why I would run down to their house at odd times of day and night – sometimes I would arrive in my nightgown. The welcome was always the same – hugs, kisses, and bread-and-butter with sugar. Mamo never hugged me, her only sign of affection was a light peck on the cheek before I climbed the ladder to the cockloft. But Dyta would embrace me, much too tightly. I hated it. He would push his rough old hand under my dress, tickle my bottom, and fondle my cuckoo until it hurt. I would cry out loudly from the pain of it. He would then push me aside roughly and say, 'Damn you, get out of my sight, you little devil.'

I would have given the whole world to have been able to live with Sara and Mari.

I was born a few months before the war broke out – the Kaiser's war, and the first recollection I had of that war was seeing a soldier outside our house, calling 'Myfanwy'. I remember it well. He was a tall, handsome man in uniform, riding a black horse. When Mamo saw him she rushed towards him excitedly, and they embraced and kissed in silence for a long, long time. I gazed at them in awe.

'What about the child?' said the man.

'She is too young to understand,' said Mamo, and carried on with their hugging.

Finally he departed, and his last words were, 'When the war is over we shall have to face the truth, and start life anew.'

'Too late, John,' said Mamo, 'too late,' and cried as if her heart would break.

At long last she controlled herself, grasped me tightly, and said, still weeping, 'Jini, you are not to tell anybody, not anybody, about what has happened today. Not on your life. Not a word to Dyta, nor to anyone else. Do you understand? Do you promise?'

'Yes, Mamo, I promise.'

Although I was so very young, I had an unhappy feeling inside me – a feeling that Dyta should be told about it. But a promise is a promise.

2

Mamo continued to weep for a long, long time and seeing Mamo weeping so pitifully made me want to weep too. It is depressing to cry, without having a reason for doing so, and when I could not stick it any longer, I went to Glan-dŵr for something to eat. I knew I could have bread-and-butter and sugar to eat there. It was quite hopeless to expect Mamo, in her present state, to cook any sort of meal.

Sara and Mari never used to ask me about anyone who visited us, but today their first question was:

'Did you have a visitor this morning?'

I was taken aback; had I not promised Mamo faithfully not to say one word about the stranger who called that morning? Suddenly I had an idea:

'A horse called to see Mamo this morning and she has been sobbing ever since.'

Mamo had not asked me to keep quiet about the horse.

'Your mother, poor dear, she's paying a heavy price for her sin,' said Mari.

'Shut up!' said Sara sharply.

Grown-up language was a mystery to me.

When I returned home later, Mamo was

peeling potatoes for supper, but her eyes were still red and swollen. She was very subdued, sniffling occasionally, and so she remained until Dyta arrived home. He sensed there was something wrong immediately:

'What the hell is wrong with you? Who's trodden on your bloody toes today?'

She ignored him, and away he went on his bike, without washing or eating, and I knew that he would not return until long past my bed-time. After he went, Mamo had another bout of crying; loudly and hysterically this time. I had never seen her like that before. Poor Mamo. I am sure it had something to do with the 'sin' that Mari had mentioned.

After a while, the sighs and hysterics subsided, and I returned to ask her, 'Mamo, what is "sin"?'

'Who has been talking to you?' she asked sharply.

'I overheard Sara and Mari talking.'

'What did they say?'

I remembered in time that I had mentioned the horse, so I had to think of a lie, and that very quickly.

'They were talking about the red cockerel,' said I looking downwards, too ashamed to look her straight in the eye.

'Mamo, what is "sin"?' I repeated. I had to know.

'Sin,' she said slowly, 'is behaving badly, doing something which is very, very wrong, something you will regret having done all the days of your life.'

I was none the wiser. I did not dare ask Dyta, in case the story of the stranger and the horse slipped out.

The man on horseback, the man called John, had upset Mamo dreadfully. She spent the following days in bed most of the time, weeping silently, and eating very little. Dyta stayed away until late every night. He was fed up with Mamo and her tantrums. So was I. Had it not been for Sara and Mari, I would have starved. It was to Glan-dŵr that I went for my breakfast of bread and milk, and I would stay for my lunch of *cawl* made with fresh vegetables. The farmer on whose land they lived allowed them to plant a row of potatoes and carrots in his field every year, in exchange for help with the harvest. They grew all sorts of herbs in their own garden. Their *cawl* was a treat.

On my way down to Glan-dŵr, I would pick wild flowers from the hedgerows. Mari knew each flower by more than one name, and knew moreover their medicinal properties. She was forever concocting ointments, and medicines for various maladies, and people would come from far and wide to be cured. I would often accompany her on her walks, gathering plants, and even help her with the mixing of the medicines, but she would never let on the name of the fluid she used as a thinning agent. That was a deep secret. I learnt that parsley was good for easy peeing, watercress for purifying the blood, and feverfew for headaches. Every so often we would wander through the fields and search the hedgerows for plants essential for the cure of yellow jaundice. There was good money in this, a shilling for a small bottle, and eighteen pence for a large one. Dr Powell of Newcastle Emlyn used to advise anyone who suffered from jaundice to visit Mari Rees.

We would walk for miles gathering plants, and Mari knew exactly where to find each one – wild tansy, rock cress, betony, buck bean, comfrey, and many, many more.

The farmers and the landowners had given her permission to wander over their land, wherever and whenever she wished. Everyone knew her, and everyone greeted her. We used to take a can of milk, a chunk of bread and a piece of cheese to eat on our way, and we would roam for a whole day from morning to night, through fields, over hedges and through marshlands. To pick the buck bean, we had to climb a hill, and then walk down to the valley on the other side to find it.

One day we met a gentleman riding a white horse. He wore a top hat, and sported a white beard. He was different from anyone I had seen before; he was a real gentleman, and had such a kind face.

'Well, Mari,' he said, 'still at it collecting plants to cure the sick. And who is this pretty little girl accompanying you?'

Mari appeared to hesitate before replying, so I spoke up for myself:

'I am Jini John, and I live at Llety'r Wennol.'

He glared at me for a second, slapped his horse and galloped away.

'Who was that man, Mari?'

'He is the gentleman who lives in the big house in the trees the other side of the river.'

'He doesn't like children, Mari.'

'Don't worry, Jini dear, he has had a great deal of worry and disappointment in life, and he can never forgive or forget.'

And I'd thought he was such a kind, noble gentleman, but he was a haughty old man, and I never wanted to see him again.

3

I had a dreadful feeling, which lingered inside me continually, a feeling that Mamo did not love me. I felt unwanted. She never praised me, never hugged me, never kissed me.

'Out of my way, Jini.'

'Sit still, Jini.'

'Shut up, for goodness' sake.'

'Go outside.'

And out I would go to Glan-dŵr to be pampered and have a bite to eat. They had neither toys nor books, apart from the Big Bible, the Hymn Book, and a beautifully-bound red book whch they called the Doctor's Book. According to Mari, this book was unique: the only book of its kind in the whole country. Sometimes when they were not around, I would take a peep at its contents. It frightened me – pictures of bones and skeletons, and even pictures of men and women without a stitch on. There were also pictures of flowers and plants, and if Mari was in a good mood, she would teach me their names, and also their medicinal value. Apparently every little weed had its purpose, and God had planted each and every one in order to help mankind.

I would spend hours gazing in fascination at the beautiful pictures in the Big Bible. Sara would narrate the stories, and explain the pictures vividly and dramatically, starting at the Garden of Eden. I wept when I heard the story of Cain killing his brother Abel, but enjoyed hearing of Esther, the brave girl who was prepared to die for her country. I decided there and then that I would one day join the army and fight for my country.

'Are girls allowed to join the army, Sara?'

'Yes, in a way, but only at home, not overseas. Our soldiers do not fight for Wales, they fight for the King and Great Britain.'

I did not knew the difference between Wales and Great Britain, and I was under the impression that our soldiers fought for Lloyd George and not the King. Nor was Sara prepared to explain.

'You ask too many questions, Jini *fach*.'

I knew when to shut up.

It was Sara who taught me to read and to write, and that was before I was three years of age. Writing on a slate, using a stone as a pencil, she would write names of people I knew on the slate – JINI, SARA, MARI, DYTA, MAMO. I learnt to read from the Big Bible. She chose easy verses at first, for example *DUW CARIAD YW* – God is love. Learning came easily. I had no trouble at all. But I found that

Bible boring. Learning to read it was fairly easy, but understanding what I had read was beyond me. Listening to Sara narrating the same tales over and over again was pure joy, but she refused to answer most of my questions 'because you are too young to understand'.

There was a picture of Jesus Christ ascending to heaven, flying with a pair of wings, bare-footed, wearing a long white robe, and a crown of thorns on his head. He looked tired and miserable. Sara said that each one of us would one day ascend to heaven.

I wanted to know more.

'Will we fly through the sky wearing a crown?'

'Not quite like that.'

'How?'

'Well . . .' Sara would always pause before answering, especially when she didn't quite know what to say. 'Well,' she said once more, 'not quite like that.'

'How?' I could see by her face that she was in a quandary. 'How, Sara?' I was determined to find out.

'First of all we will die.'

'Yes, and what then?'

'We shall be buried.'

'Buried in the garden, like Fanny the hen?'

'No, no, not in the garden, but in a graveyard, in a coffin.'

'What is a coffin?'

'A big wooden box, with a heavy lid.'

'How can we fly through the sky if we are shut up in a box, and buried in the ground?'

'Jini, you ask too many questions, you are too young to understand – you must wait until you are a big girl.'

'And when will that be?'

'When you go to school.'

That was that. I was told no more. Moreover, I did not want to go to school. I preferred to stay at home, or rather at Glan-dŵr listening to Sara's wonderful tales of Adam and Eve, of Esther, and of Moses being found in the rushes by the beautiful princess with the long black tresses, who wore a blue frock.

But I was nearly five, and I would have to go to school soon, and walk two miles each way. I knew no other child; I had never played with any child. I had never attended a Sunday school. Sara had asked Mamo, more than once, if she could take me, but no, Mamo was adamant.

'I am a Church person, and Jini was christened in Church, and if the Church were nearer, she would be attending that Sunday school.'

No one argued with Mamo. She had an 'I-know-best' attitude which put an end to all argument. Dyta was the only person who dared to contradict her. He would curse and rant but to no purpose. She would turn her back and close her lips tightly. More than once he raised his fists in anger, but she would turn to face him, and look him straight in the eye. That look would completely unnerve him. He would turn away sheepishly, go out, bang the door, take his bike, ride away, and not return until very late the following morning.

Neighbours rarely called at our house. Sara called sometimes, but she always had a reason for doing so, and she never stayed longer than a few minutes. Glan-dŵr was different, friends and neighbours were always welcome; there was a cup of tea for them whenever they called, in spite of the scarcity caused by rationing. They were always complaining about the lack of sugar: Sara blaming Mari for using sugar in her medical concoctions, and Mari insisting that sugar was essential to mitigate the bitterness of the wormwood. They never complained about the sugar they spread on my bread-and-butter. At home, Mamo never put sugar in her tea, I drank milk, but Dyta put three teaspoonfuls in his cup, and drank three cups at every sitting. Mamo sometimes used sugar to sweeten the stewed fruit, but never more than a spoonful or so.

One day I saw my chance to help Sara and Mari – the sugar container was full right to the top. I poured most of it into a paper bag, and ran full-pelt to Glan-dŵr.

'Mamo wants you to have this sugar.'

'Are you quite sure, Jini? Did your mother say so?'

I had to tell a lie. 'Dyta is the only person in our house who takes sugar.'

'She is so very kind. Please thank her on our behalf.'

But that do-good feeling did not last long. When I arrived home Mamo was preparing supper, and she had poured what remained on the stewed plums. It was an empty tin that faced Dyta.

'Where 'as the bloody sugar gone? The tin was full this morning.'

Mamo explained quietly about the sour plums, and about the little that was left in the tin.

'Bloody hell,' said Dyta, stamping and raging in a wild temper. 'What's going on in this house. Who stole the fuckin' sugar?'

'I didn't steal the fuckin' sugar,' said I, finding it rather difficult to lie this time.

'Jini,' said Mamo angrily, 'never let me hear you using that dreadful language again,' – staring hard at Dyta at the same time.

'Jini,' bellowed Dyta, 'you are lying, you little bitch. Where is the fuckin' sugar? The truth, you little liar.'

18

I was caught in a trap.

'I gave it to Sara Rees.'

'Why they hell did you give the sugar to that old witch? You must be punished mi-lady. Out to the garden.'

He dragged me out by the scruff of my neck. I was shaking like a leaf in a storm.

'Take your bloomers down. I am going to cut a stick.'

I knew what to expect. I was too scared to move. Never in my life had I received a beating on my bare bottom.

I started to shout and scream, the tears were streaming down my face. I was paralysed. I could not move, and was so ashamed.

Soon he returned carrying a tiny leafy branch. But his manner had completely changed, he was now a smiling, kind man. He took my bloomers down very gently, and asked me to lie face down across an old box. I was still crying, kicking, and shaking with my bare bottom waiting for the punishment. But to my disgust, he started to kiss my bottom like someone deranged. They were not gentle kisses, it was as if he were eating me alive. I was in pain, it was a most dreadful experience.

'Dyta, Dyta, stop, stop, you are hurting me. He didn't seem to hear me, so I continued to howl and scream at the top of my voice. Mamo must have heard me. She came to the door and shouted, 'Ifan, that's enough.'

He stopped suddenly and said, 'Pull up your bloomers and stop your bloody howling.'

But I could not stop. It came from inside, from the pit of my stomach.

I could not return to the house. I was still trembling, and too ashamed to meet Dyta face to face. A blow with a stick would have been easier to bear.

I ran to Glan-dŵr, still crying and heaving. I could not stop myself. Sara's embrace and her 'There, there, don't worry, *cariad*' helped a little. But I just could not tell them what had happened, and they didn't ask. I felt so ashamed, not only of myself, but of Dyta too.

I determined there and then that I would never, never tell another lie, as long as I lived.

4

Now and again Marged would pay us a visit –
always with a basketful of goodies, and always
with something special for me – sweets or a
handkerchief. She would arrive in the morning
having ridden on John the Poultry's cart. John
travelled around the countryside buying eggs
and chickens from the farmers to re-sell at
Newcastle Emlyn market the following Friday.
Marged would stay all day, and return during
late afternoon on John's cart.

Marged was a dear old woman, always
dressed from top to toe in black. She wore a
tiny round hat – not unlike an overgrown cork,
a black shawl flung around her shoulders, and
a black skirt trailing to the ground. She was
forever smiling, her blue eyes twinkling, and,
most important of all, she persuaded Mamo to
smile too. She called me Jane, never Jini, and
Mamo, Miss Myfanwy. Mamo objected to the
Miss, but Marged took no notice.

'Listen, Marged, I beg of you to drop the
Miss. Those days have gone for ever.'

'Nonsense, Miss Myfanwy, they will return
again, I'm certain of it.'

'Please, Marged, forget the past, it is dead

and buried. And how is HE? Does HE know about your visit here today?'

'I don't know; he doesn't ask, and I keep dumb. But I am certain he suspects. He saw me slicing the ham, and did not question me. It is wiser to shut up, and say nothing.'

'What about the rations?'

'We have plenty of everything, apart from sugar. And that will be scarcer than ever now, because Sam and Dan have had their calling-up papers. The maids and myself will have to turn to, and give a hand with the milking, unless we can have a Land Army Sub to help us. This war goes on and on – it's disheartening.'

'It won't be long now, Marged, with Lloyd George at the helm. Ifan talks about volunteering.'

'Good news, indeed. The discipline will do him the world of good. The war will soon be over then.'

Mamo gave one of her rare smiles. It was good to have Marged around.

'How does his High and Mightiness treat you these days? Still tippling and ranting?'

Mamo did not reply; she pursed her lips and the sad look returned. I enjoyed listening to them, and tried to guess who the 'HE' that they referred to was. I knew it was hopeless to ask questions.

Every time Marged arrived we had a slap-up

meal – fried ham and eggs, fresh vegetables, and apple tart, with thick cream, for pudding. Marged's day was a good day indeed. About three o'clock, we would accompany Marged to the end of the lane to meet John the Poultry; Marged always tripping over her long skirt, trying to hide her legs, whilst climbing over the cart shaft. It was really funny; then John would shout 'gee-up' and off they would canter, still laughing and waving.

When Dyta arrived home the smile disappeared, and her lips closed tightly – like a cockle shell. Dyta would always sense Marged's visit. I expect the smell of the cooking still hovered around.

'Did the old witch pay you a visit today?'

'Marged was here.'

'And what did she have today in her basket for Miss Myfanwy?'

'More than you deserve.'

'Come on Fan, out with the frying pan. I'm ready for a slice of ham.'

'Did they not give you supper tonight?'

'Yes, if you can call a bloody boiled egg supper.'

Then he would carry on gobbling his second supper noisily.

Dyta was a farm servant – he would rise early every morning to work at a farm called Rhyd-lwyd, returning home after his supper carrying a bottle of milk in his pocket, as part payment of his wages, and stinking of stale sweat and animal dung. He would then wash in an enamel bowl in the out-house, taking care to wash under his arm-pits and behind his ears. That was most important 'because the dirt and the germs always lingered in those secret places'. Then off he would go on his bike to some place unknown to us.

'Where does Dyta go every night?'

'God only knows.'

Sometimes I would be wide awake when he came home. I could hear the slightest sound from my loft. Mamo too would always be in bed long before he would arrive, and I could hear the quarrelling and the nagging.

Dyta would raise his voice in anger, and shout.

'Don't pretend to be asleep, wake up, and open your bloody legs.'

Then the bed would shake and the springs would squeak. For a short while, there would be complete silence, and then Mamo would cry as if her heart would break. She must have suffered terribly, because Mamo never cried without cause.

Dyta would not even allow her to cry, and he would shout impatiently.

'Stop your snuffling, you bloody cow. Go to

sleep so that you can get up to cook my breakfast in the morning.'

I could never sleep until all was quiet down below. And I never knew the reason for her misery, but I was certain that Dyta was the cause of it all.

I would ask her in the morning, 'Do you feel better today, Mamo?'

'What do you mean? I haven't been ill.'

'But I heard you crying last night.'

No reply, just a tightening of the mouth.

'Did Dyta hurt you last night?'

Still no reply, but I noticed the sadness in her face.

'Jini, go out to play, but be very careful not to mention to anyone about what you hear and see in this house. Understand?'

Never, never would I mention to Sara and Mari anything about the goings on in our household. It was our business, and ours alone. And to give them credit, they would never ask, nor drop hints.

But I worried all the time, though I did my best to hide my feelings. I was so worried about Mamo; why did she keep on crying in bed at night? Worried too about Dyta cursing and ranting continuously. My other great worry was that I was to start school in the spring.

So off I would run to Glan-dŵr, where my

worries did not trouble me to the same extent. But they could read my mood like a book.

'What's wrong, Jini *fach*? Have you been a naughty girl?'

'No Mari, I'm fretting.'

'You are too young to fret, Jini. Fretting about what, for goodness' sake?'

'Fretting about going to school. I am so afraid of the big boys. I saw them fighting by the bridge, when I went with Marged to the shop.'

'Don't worry, they were only playing around. They never take any notice of little girls.'

'I'm scared, Mari,' and I started to cry – the sort of crying you cannot control; an ugly sort of crying that starts down in the tummy and takes over completely. The endearments and the peppermints helped, but I could never tell them the truth, the whole truth. I had a far greater worry than that of the big boys. Dyta was my biggest worry. I was quite certain that he abused Mamo, especially at dead of night.

But I felt much better after that deep-down cry, and when I arrived home, Auntie Mary had arrived and she and Mamo were drinking tea from the best china cups, but sadly Mamo's eyes were still red and swollen.

Auntie Mary was a darling, always smiling, always talking, and always bringing me small presents. She and Mamo shared so many secrets: they laughed together, wept together and spoke English when I was not around. They thought that I could not understand, but I soon picked it up, I learnt to approach quietly, and listen outside the door, but unfortunately I could not always follow, because I didn't know the people they were talking about.

They spoke a great deal about Alun and John and an unknown person whom they called HE. Auntie Mary had nothing good to say of Dyta – she called him a 'womaniser' and a 'sot'. I had no idea what those words meant. But I gathered that she did not have one grain of respect for him.

Neither did I.

5

They said Lloyd George was going to end the war before Christmas, but he didn't. Sugar was still rationed and Dai Tan-y-fron was killed in France. Jack Llain-wen was held prisoner of war by the Germans; his mother, poor dab, cried herself sick, and blamed Lloyd George for all the killing and fighting.

Dyta spoke continuously about joining the army. Mamo kept silent, but I am certain she would have been glad to see the back of him, because she still suffered from those awful bouts of crying at dead of night. But she never complained. During the day she would remain so quiet, so very quiet, and when asked, all she would say was, 'Don't Jini, shut up Jini, go outside.'

That was all I had, day after day after day.

'Mamo, don't you like me anymore?'

'Don't be silly, child, of course I like you.'

'Why don't you speak to me, then?'

'You are too young to understand, Jini *fach*.'

No, I did not understand, but I would have loved a 'come to me, *cariad*' and a cuddle occasionally.

Everybody talked about the Germans, and everybody hated them. And if our boys had not gone out to France to fight them, they would have entered our country, and killed us all off like flies, every jack-one of us. There would be no living thing left in this country, apart from the wild animals, and a few stray dogs and cats. Every stranger was a German –

'Jini, you must never walk in the wood at the back of the house; there are Germans with guns hiding behind the bushes up there.'

'Jini, blow your nose, it is clogged up with Germans.'

It was said that the Germans had slaughtered all our boys and left them to rot on the ground in a place called the Somme. It was a time of dread and sorrow.

Early one morning Auntie Mary arrived. She tied Flower, the pony, to the gate-post, and walked slowly and downcast towards the house.

'Is your mother inside?'

I followed her into the house, sensing that something awful and unusual had happened.

She stood in the kitchen door, saying nothing, but looking so sad and pale. Mamo saw her, and realised immediately that she was the carrier of bad news.

'Mary,' she gasped, 'something terrible has happened. I want the truth, Mary, the truth.'

'John is missing.'

Mamo stifled a cry, and changed colour.

'Listen, Myfanwy, he is reported *missing*, not killed.'

'The truth, Mary. Was he not at the Somme? And all those who fought there have been wiped out?'

She leaned on the table – she actually spread herself across the table and uttered a weird cry, a dreadful sound, more like the howl of a dog then a human sound. It frightened me and I remembered that John was the name of the stranger on horseback who paid Mamo a visit a long time ago – the man whose visit was a deep secret.

'Jini, go out to play,' said Auntie Mary.

Out to play? Play with what, and with whom? So off I went to Glan-dŵr, feeling unloved and unwanted. There I would be spoilt and pampered.

'You're early this morning, Jini. Anything wrong?'

'Auntie Mary has arrived with news that John is missing. Do you know who John is?'

They looked at each other in dismay and shock.

'There is more than one John, Jini. John is a very common name.'

'But Mamo is upset over this John, and she is crying pitifully.'

'Come on, Jini. Which do you prefer? Honey or sugar on your bread?'

That was final – no more questions. I knew when to shut up. There I stayed all day long, helping Mari to brew a herbal drink.

'Jini, it is seven o'clock, you had better go home, your mother will be worried about you.'

'No-one worries about me, Mari. Mamo won't even speak to me.'

But home I had to go, sad and unwillingly – home where no-one spoke to me or kissed me.

I shall never forget the look on Mamo's face at that moment. Her whole appearance was ghastly. Her long black tresses were hanging in strands around her shoulders, her face was ashen grey, and the tears were streaming down her cheeks. She looked older even than Marged. Poor Mamo! I had to say something.

'Who is John, Mamo?'

'Shut up, Jini – it is no-one you know.'

'Is John dead, Mamo?'

'I don't know – don't ask me any more questions.'

At that moment Dyta arrived. He took one look at Mamo.

'What the hell has been churning you?'

Mamo did not reply.

'Who was here today?'

'Auntie Mary came this morning,' said I, glad of something to say.

'Oh, I see. So you have heard the latest.'

Not a word from Mamo.

'Oh yes, I also heard the news. John Coedperthi, that good-for-nothing upstart, has been killed, so it seems. Good riddance – one bugger less in this world to trample on the workers.'

Mamo straightened herself, brushed away her tears, and screamed in a hard, harsh voice:

'Don't you ever speak about John in that way again. You are not fit to lick his boots. John was a brave man, not an underhand coward like you, who finds all manner of petty excuses to avoid joining the army. You make me sick. John was worth a dozen of your sort – you useless weakling.'

'But it was me you bloody well married.'

'Yes, more to my shame. A life-sentence would have been easier to bear, than the punishment I have to suffer married to you. Get out of my sight you – you maggot. Out!'

And out he went, quietly – a man subdued.

Never had I seen Mamo in such a wild state, and never had I seen Dyta so shocked and speechless. His mouth was open wide, but no words came. Mamo's eyes were flashing, and her hair was flying untidily about her head and shoulders. She reminded me of the old gipsy who used to travel around selling pegs and telling one's fortune.

Dyta left to seek comfort elsewhere – there was no comfort for anyone at Llety'r Wennol that night. Mamo went to bed without even bidding me good-night, her hair hanging down, her face pale and unwashed. She was not the Mamo I knew. She had changed in one day from being a beautiful woman to an old hag. I did not recognise her anymore.

I drank my nightly cup of milk, and climbed the ladder to the cockloft. I could not sleep, my mother's sobs kept me awake all night. I tossed and I turned, and tried to make sense of the day's upheaval. Who was John? And why was Mamo so upset.

I got up early, and took her a cup of tea. The tears and the sobs had stopped, but she refused to talk to me. She did not even thank me for the tea.

Dyta stayed away all night, neither did he return in the morning. I did not go to Glan-dŵr that day – I felt I could not leave Mamo on her own.

The postman seldom called at our house but he came that day.

'Is your father at home?'

'No.'

'Is your mother at home?'

'Yes, but she is in bed, very ill, and not able to speak.'

'I have an important letter here for your father, and it must be signed for. Can you write?'

'Yes, of course.'

'What is your name?'

'Jini John.'

'Write your name on this line, in your best writing.'

I did my very best, just as Sara had taught me.

'Good girl. Give this letter to your father as soon as he comes back.'

It was a long brown envelope with O.H.M.S. clearly stamped on it.

'Mamo, there is a letter for Dyta.'

'Give it to me.'

She just glanced at it and said, 'Thank heaven, it will give me great pleasure to give your father this.'

She would never refer to him as 'Dyta', always 'your father'.

And indeed after receiving the letter she got up, washed, combed her hair and prepared a meal. But she still looked old and drawn, and spoke not a word.

I was outside when Dyta arrived. I met him at the gate.

'There is an important letter for you, Dyta.'

He rushed to the house, but Mamo was ready for him.

'A letter for you, Ifan.'

He gazed in awe at the letter. Then the truth dawned upon him.

'Who signed for this bloody letter?'

'Me,' feeling proud of myself.

Mamo half smiled, as if she had forgotten her sorrow for a second. Dyta tore the envelope open, and gazed open-mouthed at the contents.

'The buggers.'

'Who are they?' asked Mamo quietly.

'Jenkins and his bloody sons. They have managed between them to keep those two bastards out of the army. It is me who has to face the bloody Germans.'

'But I thought you were keen to join the army.'

'You would be glad to see me dead wouldn't you? You bitch.'

Mamo did not reply. Although I did not like Dyta, I did not want him to be killed. I did not like to hear of anybody or anything being killed. I was afraid of death.

And away went Dyta on his bike without washing or shaving, and I was bold enough to ask him. 'Where are you off to, Dyta?'

'Anywhere to bury my sorrows, and as far as I possibly can from that mother of yours.'

He looked wild and dishevelled. Mamo watched him from the window, and there was a shadow of a smirk hovering around her lips.

6

Two days later, Dyta disappeared again; I didn't know where or why he went. But when he returned he looked so miserable and down-hearted, but cleaner and tidier than I had seen him for a long time.

'Did you pass?' asked Mamo quietly.

'Yes, I bloody well passed. A1 – to hell with it! No doubt, you will be bloomin' glad to hear that I will have to go next Friday.'

'Oh!'

'Is that all you have to say?'

'What is there to say?'

'You're jolly fuckin' glad aren't you? You'd love to hear of my death, wouldn't you, wouldn't you?'

Mamo's lips tightened, and her eyes flashed, but she kept quiet.

'I'm fed up – I'm going out – out of this bloody hell. Life in the army can't be worse than what I 'ave to suffer here.'

'But will you be able to escape so easily from that other hell?' she replied with a sly smile.

Dyta had to shut up. Mamo beat him every time in an argument. Off he went as usual, on his bike with his tail between his legs.

He did not return for several days, and when he did he was dressed in his brand new uniform.

36

He was a different man, his puttees wound tightly round his legs, his buttons shining, his boots squeaking, and his hair closely cropped. I had a shock. He looked so different, so smart, and I believe Mamo was surprised too.

That night there was a concert held in his honour at the school. It was called a 'farewell concert', because he was leaving for France before the end of the week. And to my joy I was allowed to go. I had not the faintest idea what a concert was, and I was anxious to know. Mamo refused to come.

'It is too far to walk, and I cannot abide listening to a crowd of women singing and squealing out of tune like a litter of pigs.'

I rode on the bar of the bike, a most uncomfortable ride with Dyta breathing down my neck all the way.

I saw the school for the first time: it was chock-a-block with people shouting and clapping and as we entered they all sang in chorus:

Ifan John is off to fight,
    Hurrah! Hurrah!
To chase all the Germans out of sight,
    Hurrah! Hurrah!
Soon Ifan will come home again,
    Hurrah! Hurrah!
And all the Germans dead – Amen
Hurrah! Hurrah!

Then they all stood up, and carried on shouting 'Hurrah! Hurrah!' for a long, long time, just shouting for the sake of shouting. The noise was deafening. When they finally stopped, a few children sang and recited, a few forgot their lines, then started all over again; men cracking jokes which I could not understand; men and women half singing and half screaming (Mamo was quite right, they did sound like pigs squealing). It was great fun, and I did enjoy myself.

Before the end, two men passed around their black bowler hats for the collection, and they handed it over to Dyta. His pockets were bursting with money, and it was all his. I couldn't understand why Mamo refused to come.

When we arrived home, Mamo was in bed; I too prepared myself for the loft, but suddenly Dyta caught hold of me, clutched me in his arms and kissed me wildly. He pressed me so roughly against him that I nearly lost my breath. I could feel his brass buttons hard against my breast. He lifted my frock and kissed my bare skin. I was on the point of screaming, but he put his hand across my mouth. Then he changed completely, and in a quiet voice said, 'Please, Jini *fach*, be a good girl whilst I'm away, and never forget your Dyta. You're Dyta's girl, Jini, and don't you listen to old women's gossip about me.'

I must say that I felt just a little bit sorry that

he had to join the army, but I did hate all that kissing and fondling. Did all fathers behave like that towards their children?

I went to bed dead tired, but before I dropped off to sleep, I remembered to say my prayers – the prayers that Sara had taught me.

Now I lay me down to sleep,
I pray the Lord my soul to keep,
If I should die before I wake,
I pray the Lord my soul to take. Amen.

Tonight I added my own bit to it – I wanted Jesus to know that Dyta had joined the army.

Ifan John has gone to fight,
Hurrah! Hurrah!
– and please Jesus Christ to be good to him,
 and bring him home safely. Amen.

Although I was dead tired, I did not fall asleep for a long, long time. I kept thinking of Dyta leaving at five in the morning, perhaps for ever. Not every soldier returns from the war. I re-lived the concert, and felt guilty that I had enjoyed myself so much. Then I heard the bed shaking and clattering, followed by Mamo's sobbing. Why? I could not understand. Finally I slept, and I did not hear Dyta leaving at break of day. I don't think Mamo did either.

When I got up, the sun was shining. Dyta had left, and Mamo was in a better mood than I had seen her for a long time.

Auntie Mary arrived during the afternoon, complete with some fancy cakes and a jar of rhubarb jam. Mamo spread the lace cloth on the table, brought out the best dishes – the pink ones edged with gold, and we drank tea from the china tea-pot, not the old brown pot with the cracked spout. We did enjoy ourselves; Mamo was rather subdued, but she smiled at Auntie Mary's jokes – not the sly smile of the tight lips – but a broad smile that lit up her whole face. I tried my best to appear happy and that I was enjoying myself, but there was a bogey-man hovering above me constantly, and the fact that I would have to start school at Easter.

'Don't worry, Jini *fach*,' said Auntie Mary, 'children enjoy going to school.'

'I shan't enjoy.'

'You won't, if you are determined not to.'

Thereupon I started to sniffle – I had a job to force the tears, but they appeared eventually. I knew full well how to win Auntie Mary's sympathy. But it did not work this time, and the following week I had to face the great wide world, all on my own.

As usual I ran to Glan-dŵr to pour out my troubles.

'I shall accompany you all the way,' said Sara, 'and what is more, I am prepared to stay at school with you all day long.'

'No, the children will think I am no better than a baby doll. You shall come as far as the school gate, and no further.'

And so it happened. Marged had presented me with a brand new school-bag to carry my bottle of milk and bread-and-butter, and away we went, Sara and I, on the first Monday after Easter, walking the two miles, in the pouring rain.

'I'm tired, Sara. I want to go home.'

'Come on, buck up. I can hear the sound of children.'

And lo and behold, the road was crowded with children of all shapes and sizes, laughing and screaming, and the sound of their clogs battering the stony ground. I wore boots – a present from Auntie Mary.'

'Children who are well-brought up never wear clogs. Don't ever wear clogs, Jini,' she said.

I didn't know any of the children, but a big, strapping girl came and took hold of my hand and said, 'You may go home now, Miss Rees. I'll look after Jini.'

I had no idea how she knew me, because I had never seen her before, but I felt happier having met Hannah Tan-rhiw.

'Come and play "calico she" with me?'

'What is that?'

'Just look at them, they are all playing "calico she".' Two children clasped hands from behind, then they ran together shouting at the top of their voices,

'Calico she, calico she,

Turn around the robin du.'

Then suddenly they dropped hands, turned around quickly, exchanged places, and started again from the beginning. I soon got the gist of it, but I found it rather difficult, because Hannah was much taller than I was – we did not fit together. But it was great fun, and a good way to arrive in school, without dawdling on the way.

We were early and played in the school-yard for a while; Hannah looking after me, not unlike the red cockerel guarding his hens back at Glan-dŵr. Then a bell was rung, and we all ran to 'lines'.

'You must join the "babies" now. I shall see you at the "small playtime",' said Hannah, and away she went.

I felt frightened and nervous. I followed the 'babies', and I found myself standing on my own in front of a noisy class. I had no idea what to do, what to say, or where to go. All the other children ran to their desks. A tall gawky woman, wearing spectacles, looked down snootily at me, and said in English, 'And who on earth are you?'

'Jini John.'

'Jini John, *Miss*. You must address me as "Miss" at all times. And don't you ever forget that, Jini John.'

'Please Miss, please Miss, please Miss,' shouted a girl with red hair.

'And what do you want, Mary Anne?'

'Please Miss, please Miss, she can sit next to me. She is my sister, Miss.'

'Don't be ridiculous, child.'

'Yes Miss, indeed Miss, my mother told me, Miss.'

I opened my mouth nervously and said, 'I have no sister.'

At that the tall, thin woman, grasped my arm, and gave me a good shaking.

'You must always call me "Miss". Do you understand, you naughty child. Always "Miss".'

'Yes, miss,' and the tears started to roll down my cheeks – real tears, genuine tears. I noticed a quiet little boy sitting on his own at the back of the class, and looking lonely and unhappy like myself.

'I will sit next to that boy in the corner.'

At this, all the children gave out a roar of laughter, exactly as if I had cracked a huge joke.

'You are talking nonsense, child. He is a German.'

I was shocked, for I had been told so many times that every German was dangerous, and that every German should be shot. But this little boy looked so harmless, so like every other child.

At long last I had a seat right in front of the class, right under Miss's nose.

Then the register was called. Miss called out each child's name in a high, raucous voice, and each child shouted in reply.

'Present, Miss Jones Parry, Miss.'

I felt glad that Mamo had taught me to speak English, because Miss seemed unable to speak any Welsh. Dyta was very angry at Mamo for talking to me in English now and again:

'Hell's bells, why do you have to teach the girl the lingo of the bloody English – the lingo of the bloomin' snobs?'

'She might be glad of it one day,' she would answer quietly. Mamo was right, of course.

Then suddenly I heard Miss Jones Parry's high-pitched voice shouting.

'What is your name child?'

'Jini John, Miss.'

'What a funny name. Your name in full, child?'

'Mary Ann Jane John, Miss.'

'And your date of birth?'

'April, Miss.'

44

'Ask your mother to write the date on this paper, and bring it back tomorrow.'

I took the paper and sat down, feeling like a frightened little rabbit caught in a trap. Miss mounted on a high stool, cried out, 'Silence! Repeat your tables.'

In one loud chorus they bawled.

'Twice one are two, Miss,

Twice two are four, Miss,' and on and on until they arrived at 'Twice twelve are twenty-four, Miss.'

Then they started to say the table backwards, finishing at 'Twice one are two, Miss.'

But they did not finish there, oh no. We had to go over them again, and again, and again. By the end I knew them off by heart, and I could see that everyone was really fed up; our voices had faded almost to a whisper.

But Miss continued to sit on her high stool, quite unconcerned, trimming her nails with a long file. This went on for a long, long time.

'Take out your slates, children – quietly.'

But I did not possess a slate. I sat there quietly, and said nothing. Everybody wrote busily – the stone pencils squeaking like a lot of little mice.

'Finish Miss, finish Miss,' they called out one after the other. No-one spoke quietly.

'Rub out and start again – be careful not to rub out the top line.'

Behold Mary Anne, that lump of a girl who said she was my sister, had to open her big mouth and exclaimed, 'Miss, Miss, please Miss, Jini John hasn't got a slate, Miss.'

Miss looked at me, as if she had not seen me before.

'Don't you have a tongue, child?'

'No, Miss.' I was terrified.

'What a stupid child you are.'

She went to rummage in the cupboard, and brought out a brand new slate, and a stump of a stone pencil. Clearly in chalk she wrote half a dozen letters at the top of the slate:

$$\mathcal{A} \quad \mathcal{B} \quad \mathcal{C} \quad \mathcal{D} \quad \mathcal{E} \quad \mathcal{F}$$

'Copy those to the bottom, and be careful not to blot out the top line.'

Sara had taught me how to write letters but they were different from those, and soon I had filled the whole space.

'I have finished, Miss,' feeling proud of my English and of my work.

'Rub out and start again,' she said, without even glancing at my work. That was how I spent the whole morning, rubbing out and starting again. I spat on my slate, and dried it with my sleeve, while Miss was perched on a stool cleaning her nails. I was hungry and miserable. When 'morning small play' arrived,

I thought it was dinner time, and started to eat my packed lunch, but Hannah saw me.

'Don't eat your food now – you keep that until dinner time.'

Disappointment My stomach was churning, as if it were full of live maggots, but away went Hannah to play with the big girls. The little German stood all alone in the corner of the yard, so I plucked enough courage to approach him.

'What is your name?'

'Eitel – you are Jini?'

He spoke Welsh, just like me, and I had been told that no German could speak either Welsh or English.

But Mary Anne, the red-head, appeared on the scene.

'Come, don't talk to that thing, or Miss will be very cross indeed.'

'Why? He is a nice little boy.'

'He is a German, and there are no nice Germans. They kill babies and eat them. Come and play with me – you are my sister, you know.'

Mary Anne would have been the very last person in the whole world whom I would have wished to have as a sister. I would have much preferred to have the German as a brother. The bell sounded, lines again, and back to the classroom, one behind another, like a flock of geese. Miss gave out reading books, all dirty and torn, with pages missing. We started to read.

'The cat is on the mat. The cat sits on the mat,' and on and on. Baby reading. I was used to grown-up reading like the Bible and the *Tivy-side*. Sara had taught me to read proper books. Miss continued to sit on her high stool. She had finished trimming her nails, and after listening to each child reading the same page once, she carried on reading the *Western Mail*, and ignored us.

There sat behind me a fat boy with fair hair and puffed-out red cheeks. I did not fancy his looks. He took out a rusty pen-knife from his pocket.

'See this? I shall castrate you tomorrow.'

I had no idea what he meant. He frightened me. Miss kept on reading her paper, and took no notice of us. So I decided, there and then, that I would not attend school that afternoon, nor the following day, nor the day after that. I'd had enough of school. So when dinner time arrived I grasped my new bag, ran full-pelt from Miss Jones Parry and her tatty books, determined never to return again.

I was afraid of being castrated, whatever that meant. And, moreover, neither Miss nor the school had anything at all to teach me.

7

I ran, and I ran, until I could run no more. I was clean out of breath, but I had to get away, as far as I possibly could, from Miss and from Wili Weirglodd and his alarming knife. I had no idea what 'to castrate' meant, but it could not have been anything to enjoy, or a knife would not have been necessary for the job. Ach a fi!

I sat by the hedge to eat my sandwiches, and who should come along but an old tramp. I knew Twm Trefaldwyn quite well: he was a friendly old soul, always chatting and telling stories about his old home in North Wales.

'What are you doing here, all on your own?'

'Nothing.'

'A nice little girl like you should be at school.'

'There is no school today.'

Another lie. But at times it is so much easier to lie than to tell the truth. And what business was it of his anyway?

I started to run again.

I arrived at Glan-dŵr dripping with sweat, and found Sara and Mari drinking their daily *cawl*.

'Jini! What has happened? Why aren't you at school?'

I rubbed my eyes, in an effort to produce

tears, but I did not feel miserable enough for that, because I was so happy to have escaped from Miss Jones Parry's clutches and her dreadful school.

'What is wrong, Jini *fach*?' asked Sara, so full of concern and sympathy. I could always depend on her soft heart.

'What is castrate, Sara?'

'What a funny thing to ask.'

'Wili Weirglodd is going to castrate me tomorrow.'

Silence – utter silence.

'What is "to castrate", Sara?' I asked again, raising my voice. I had to know.

'Don't worry, Jini *fach*. No-one can castrate little girls. It is impossible.'

'Why?'

No reply.

'Why? Tell me why!' I insisted.

'Well,' said Sara slowly and painfully, 'they can only castrate farm animals.'

'Sara,' said Mari quite sharply, 'don't beat about the bush, tell the child the truth.'

'If you are so knowledgeable about castration, why don't you tell her yourself,' said Sara peevishly.

There was a pause. Mari eventually cleared her throat, found her voice, stared at the basin of *cawl* in front of her, and said in a voice of authority.

'Boys are different from girls. They have a "piece" or a "spout" that sticks out in front of them.'

'Dyta has a spout,' I said, showing off my knowledge of men. But Mari was not interested in Dyta's spout.

'To castrate,' said Mari, 'is to cut off that spout, and then they become half and half – half man, half woman. Afterwards they speak in a thin, high voice. *You* needn't worry, Jini. You must have a spout before you can be castrated.'

That was a slight comfort, but that did not stop them from asking further awkward questions.

'Is that why you ran away?'

'Yes and no.'

'What's wrong, Jini *fach*?' asked Sara.

'I hate school, and I am never, ever, never, going back there again.'

'Why in heaven's name? Have you been badly treated? The truth, Jini.'

'Yes, but not half as bad as they treat the German. They treat him like dirt. And Miss calls me a "stupid child". I didn't learn anything at all, at all.'

'What do you mean, Jini?'

'We say "twice one are two, Miss" for hours on end. We read "the cat is on the mat" from a smudgy ragged book, we write funny letters on

51

the slate over and over again, while Miss, if you please, sits on a high stool reading the newspaper. I was fed up. That is why I am never going back there again. So that's that.'

They both looked at each other aghast, and eventually Mari said in a voice of authority, 'You must go to school, or else your mother will be taken to jail. The "whipper-in" will call at your house, and take your mother away.'

'What is a "whipper-in", Mari?'

'A man who visits houses, to make certain that every child attends school. The whipper-in is a nasty man.'

I had a shock. That was the first time for me to learn of the whipper-in. I felt slightly better after drinking the *cawl* and Sara and I spent the afternoon reading the *Tivy-side*. She praised me, as she always did.

'You read just as well as the vicar in the pulpit.'

Sadly, I had to return home to face the music, hoping against hope that there would be no more awkward questions. Luckily Auntie Mary was there, and they were both drinking tea – the lace cloth spread on the table, the best dishes, and lump sugar in the basin. Mamo liked a touch of style.

'Well, Jini *fach*, you are home early.'

'I ran all the way.' I did not say when.

'Did you enjoy yourself at school?'

'No.'

'Why, Jini?'

'I cannot stand Miss, and Wili Weirglodd is going to castrate me tomorrow.'

For a moment there was complete silence, then they looked at each other, and rolled with laughter.

'What is castrate, Auntie Mary?' I was beginning to enjoy myself.

'You are too young to understand about such things. Wili Weirglodd is talking a load of rubbish. He has no idea himself about what it means to castrate.'

'But he had a big knife ready for the job.'

'You must tell Miss Jones Parry about it. She will put a stop to all that.'

'Miss Jones Parry is too busy filing her nails and reading the *Western Mail*.'

Then they carried on talking in English thinking that I could not understand them. Silly fools! Thank goodness Mari had explained everything to me, but I kept on thinking about Wili Weirglodd and his knife. But it was necessary for me to prepare myself for the act, for I was quite determined not to attend school the following day. I decided to start ailing after supper, that is after I realised that there was fried pork, roast potatoes and rice pudding on the menu. I did enjoy the supper.

'Jini, get ready for bed.'

'I have a dreadful pain, Mamo. It came on very suddenly.'

'Where exactly is the pain?'

'I feel bad all over.'

'All right. You need a dose of camomile tea – that will cure it.'

I had tasted that once before; it was so awful, that I became really sick after drinking it.

'No, I'm going to bed.'

So off I went to the cock-loft. I could still hear their chat:

'You are very callous, Myfanwy; perhaps the child is really ill.'

'You don't know Jini. She is devious. She is just like her father. She is planning to stay at home tomorrow. I know her tricks.'

Mamo could think whatever she wished, but I was determined to be very sick tomorrow, and I decided on a sore throat and a headache.

Morning arrived suddenly and the first I heard was Mamo shouting, 'Jini, get up! Breakfast is ready.'

I was on the point of obeying, and suddenly I remembered.

'I am sick, Mamo.'

'Get up, at once!'

'Indeed, Mamo, I am ill, really ill. I can't even swallow my spit, and my head is splitting.'

'Jini, for the last time, get up.'

I knew when to obey. Her voice started to tremble, and that was a bad sign.

So, reluctantly, I obeyed, and summoned enough strength to refuse breakfast, although I was starving. I tried my best to squeeze a tear, but the fountain had run dry. Mamo saw that I had not touched my breakfast. She relented and said, 'All right, you may stay at home for today, but only for today. No going out, and no going to Glan-dŵr. Understand?'

'Yes, Mamo,' I replied meekly, but that was punishment, almost as bad as going to school. A miserable day, nothing to read; there was not even a Welsh Bible in the house. Nothing to play with, apart from a rag doll with the stuffing sticking out of its belly. Other children had brothers and sisters, but not me, and nearly everybody had a cat or a dog to play with, but not me. Then suddenly I remembered Mary Anne.

'Mamo.'

'Yes.'

'Do I have a sister?'

'Don't be silly, girl. Why do you ask?'

'Mary Anne said so, and she was quite certain.'

'Who on earth is Mary Anne?'

'A girl with ginger hair. She lives at Penrhiw – she is the same age as myself.'

Mamo suddenly became very quiet; she looked into the distance, bit her lip, and I could see a tear in the corner of her eye.

'Mamo, please don't upset yourself. I don't want Mary Anne as a sister – she is an ugly, fat lump of a girl.'

'Go outside and play, Jini.'

She had forgotten that I had to stay in the house, because of my 'illness'. So off I went full tilt to Glan-dŵr, where I had a lovely time playing snakes-and-ladders with Sara and telling them all about my supposed illness.

'What about your mother? Does she know you are here?'

'Mamo is sick with worry. So am I?'

'Worried about what, for goodness' sake?'

'Worried that Mary Anne might be my sister.'

'And who might Mary Anne be?'

'Mary Ann Penrhiw – the fat girl with ginger hair.'

I noticed that they both looked at each other and spoke, not with words, but with their eyes. I had noticed Mamo and Auntie Mary doing the very same thing; it was a kind of secret code.

'Don't worry about that cheeky girl; she is talking nonsense. Let us carry on with the game, and if you win, you shall stay here to eat *cawl* and rice pudding.'

I forgot about Mary Anne. But I could not get school out of my mind, and to make matters worse, Mari gave me another sermon about the result of staying at home and the threat of the whipper-in.

I supposed that I would have to obey. So I determined to be as brave as Esther in the Bible, and that I would tell Wili Weirglodd to his face to put away his knife, and that castrating little girls is impossible.

8

The threat of the 'whipper-in' weighed on me heavily. Sara and Mari never told lies – never.

So off I went, against the grain, to school, complete with a packet of sandwiches and a bottle of milk in my bag. Mamo accompanied me to the end of the lane.

'Be a good girl, Jini, and I shall cook pancakes for tea.' I loved pancakes – hot from the griddle.

Mamo was so much happier since Dyta had joined the army. So was I. No swearing, no yelling, and Mamo laughing at Marged and Auntie Mary's jokes.

I took my time to walk to school – I was in no hurry to see Miss. There was no sign of children anywhere. Then I started to hop, skip and jump to break the monotony – I could not play 'calico-she' on my own.

I was late, an unforgivable sin; they were all sitting at their desks, and blaring out the tables ('Four ones are four, Miss' today, because it was Wednesday).

'Jini John you are late. Where were you yesterday?'

'Home with a bad head.'

'Say "Miss", Jini John.'

'Miss.'

'Where is the paper I gave you?'

I had completely forgotten about the paper. I had even forgotten to give it to Mamo. And that started Miss off on a long-winded sermon about naughty children. No one would ever like me again, and nobody would ever play with me again. Never no more.

But she was very wrong, because when morning short play arrived, the big girls invited me to join them in a game called 'Roll of Tobacco'. It was a silly game. A row of children would grasp one another's hands, encircle the tall girl in the middle. Then we would jump wildly up and down, shouting at the top of our voices, 'roll of tobacco, don't fall down'. But fall down we did, huddled on top of one another on the stony playground, some laughing, some screaming, and a few of the younger ones crying. I was slightly hurt, but I did not cry. Babies cry.

I hated school, and but for playtime, life would be unbearable. The same routine day after day after day. Shouting out the tables – a different one for each day; starting at 'twice one are two, Miss' on Monday, until we eventually arrived at 'twice six are twelve, Miss' on Friday; copying the top line, the same top line every day; reading tatty books; sums suitable for babies only; and every afternoon playing with stinking green clay.

But fortunately on Tuesdays and Thursdays during the afternoons the pattern varied. Miss Evans who taught Standards I, II and III in the big room would come to the babies' class to teach us drawing.

Miss Evans was a pretty woman, with shiny black hair tied in a bun on the top of her head. She spoke quietly to us in Welsh when Miss was not around. We were allowed to draw all kinds of things – flowers and animals – she always praised us for doing our best, and never called anyone a 'stupid child'.

When the drawing lesson was over, she would read to us all kinds of tales – funny tales like the story of the three bears and the porridge, and the princess who slept for a hundred years. It was Miss Evans who told us about Dewi Sant and John Penry, of Prince Llywelyn and Owain Glyndŵr, and how the English were always fighting the Welsh.

One day, as she was showing us a picture of Dewi Sant, I read aloud the caption under it. 'Dewi Sant, the first Archbishop of Wales, and the patron saint of the Welsh people.'

'Jini,' said Miss Evans in surprise, 'you are able to read that? You should be in Standard I. I shall mention it to the Master.'

But nothing came of it. I remained in the babies' class. It was the 'Tall-thin' who was the boss, not the Head Master.

At long last the summer holidays arrived; happy days, playing in the stream, catching trout and minnows with Sara, and gathering herbs in the fields and hedgerows with Mari.

Mamo never went out visiting or shopping. Groceries were delivered to the house by a man called Willie Tom who drove a pony and cart. But after Dyta joined the army, Mamo and I would sometimes walk two miles over the hill to visit Auntie Mary, and her father Mr Puw. They lived in a big farmhouse called Pen-gwern with servants and two maids who wore lace aprons and starched caps. And there were animals everywhere – cats, dogs, horses. I did have fun, and they called Mamo 'Miss Myfanwy'.

That is what Dyta called her too, when he was in a vile temper, but the way he said it was quite different – he uttered it in a nasty, spiteful tone of voice, with the emphasis on the 'Miss'.

Mamo and Auntie Mary would saddle two ponies from the stables, and gallop over the fields. Sometimes I would be allowed to join them riding the old white pony called Flower. I was in my element; it was great to be alive during those days.

But one afternoon, having spent the day roaming the fields with Mari, I arrived home early and heard a man's voice raving and ranting in the house. He sounded just like Dyta.

He was Dyta! His boots down at heel and covered with mud. The brass buttons had lost their shine, and he had not shaved for days.

'Dyta!'

I leapt into his arms and he pressed me to his chest, very tightly until it hurt.

'Thank God, someone is glad to see me. Your mother is like a bloody stone statue.'

Yes, Mamo did appear upset. She stood stiffly, her lips tightly closed, and the smile had disappeared.

There was dead silence afterwards, apart from the sound of Dyta guzzling his ham and eggs.

I ventured to speak.

'Are you going back again, Dyta?'

'Yes love, I am going back tomorrow to God's hellfire. And you will be bloody lucky if you will ever see me again.'

After supper Dyta washed and shaved and looked more like himself.

Mamo remained sullen and dumb.

We all went to bed early. I was awake for a long, long time, listening to the bed below going clickety-clack, clickety-clack like the engine of a train. After the train stopped I could hear Mamo sobbing pitifully for a long, long time, and I could hear Dyta snoring like a pig.

9

Dyta departed the following morning, a cleaner and tidier man than he was when he arrived. I had to suffer his crushing embrace. I hated that; it made me feel sick. We accompanied him as far as the gate, but not a step further. Mamo said that she felt tired, and no wonder after the fun and games in bed the night before.

'Why was Dyta so miserable?'

'He is leaving for France tomorrow.'

Not another word.

Away I ran to Glan-dŵr.

'Your poor dad – we shall be lucky if we ever see him again.'

'Why, Sara?'

But before Sara had a chance to reply, Mari said sharply, 'Shut up, Sara. Who are you to play God? Of course we shall see him again.'

But I could not stop worrying – because I knew that soldiers were killed by the thousand in France. Tomos y Gof said so. And it was Lloyd George's fault. The two sons of Pantglas had been killed, and the Master's son was missing. I tried to be sorry for him, but I couldn't. I didn't care for him; he was a nasty man. He was also fat and pot-bellied, with a hideous moustache. The big boys used to yell a

rhyme when he was safely out of sight and
hearing.

> The master of the school,
> He is a bloody fool,
> He punches the boys with his fists,
> And the girls, he tickles their tits.
> Go to hell and good riddance.

I hated the idea of returning to school after the
holidays – repeating the tables again, and
playing with that smelly clay. That was even
worse than the torn reading books; but I was no
longer frightened of Wili Weirglodd's castrating
knife. Neither did the English that Miss spoke
worry me, and I was able to help the other
children to understand what she said.

The first day after the holidays, Miss was
dressed in black from top to toe, deep
mourning. She wiped her nose with a white
handkerchief edged with black, and spoke very
quietly. The squeak had vanished.

'Children, you must not shout or laugh
today, and you must talk very quietly, because
the Master has had terrible news. His only son
has been killed in France.'

And in we went, silently, on tip-toe – not to
the 'babies', but to the 'big room', and there we
whispered the tables. Then, Miss Evans's class
piled on us in the 'babies'. But I didn't care – to

have Miss Evans as our teacher, made up for all the disadvantages. And to crown it all, I was allowed to read with the Standard II children, and to hear Miss Evans say, 'You read better than anyone.' The world was full of joy during those days.

But it did not last long. The Master was back within a fortnight – very subdued and listless – his moustache drooping over his lower lip, his shoulders bent, and shuffling his feet. And Miss was back with the 'babies' once more, sitting on her high stool, trimming her nails. But we were not allowed to shout the tables anymore – thank goodness for that.

But one day, the unexpected happened. The Master walked into our class and announced in a voice of authority without even glancing at Miss . . . 'Jini John and Eitel Kaeseberg, you will move up to Standard I tomorrow.'

No explanation. I did not want to know why. I was only too pleased to say goodbye to Miss; her tattered books, and the smelly clay. Eitel was pleased too – he was not told to sit in the corner of Miss Evans's room. Moreover he was treated like every other child, called 'Eitel' and not the 'German'.

Unfortunately, Standards I and II occupied part of the 'big room', and the Master used to watch every move, and eavesdrop too.

Miss Evans was conscious of that; she would

turn her back to him, and try her best to ignore him. Then the Master would bellow, 'Miss Evans, speak up, your pupils cannot hear you.'

It was he who could not hear her, not the children. He was a nasty, sarcastic man. I remember Miss Evans giving us a talk on 'The Owl' (every lesson had to be taught through the medium of English). Miss Evans began in her gentle, quiet voice. 'The owl has very soft feathers'. As usual, the Master was listening and he roared in his bullock voice, 'Fluffy is the correct word to use, not soft. Use your common sense, woman.'

Miss Evans had a job to restrain the tears. He was a hateful old man. He would not have dared to speak like that to Miss.

We used to learn poetry too – both English and Welsh. My favourite was the Welsh poem called 'The Pauper's Grave'.

'Neath the sombre spreading yew tree
A grassy mound arose above the ground.

And I would weep silently, thinking that one day Twm Trefaldwyn, the drunken old tramp, would be buried under the yew tree, and as he himself would often say, 'I have no friends or relations in the whole world apart from the rabbits and the birds.'

'You have me, Twm.'

'Thank you, dear, but nobody at all will miss me.'

'I will Twm, honestly, cross my heart, fire of hell.'

And every time I recited 'The Pauper's Grave' I wept for Twm Trefaldwyn, even though he was hale and hearty, and drunk as often as possible.

Another piece that made me cry was 'Lucy Gray' –

> '. . . when I crossed the Wild,
> I chanced to see at break of day
> The solitary Child.'

At long last, attending school was joy, and I believed that there was no other person in the whole world who was so clever and so kind as Miss Evans. She was pretty too, but not quite as nice-looking as Mamo, who had big, blue eyes, and a slim, lithe figure. And since Dyta had gone to the army, she dressed nicely too, with a gold chain round her neck, and a gold watch on her wrist. Lately she had abandoned the sack apron.

Unfortunately, two afternoons a week, Miss would take over and teach the girls to sew. All we were taught was how to darn, patch and make button-holes. At the end of the year I was none the wiser, and the stitching of button-holes has remained a mystery for me all the days of my life. Her one and only instruction was 'unpick and try again'. I did just that, until my fingers bled, and the piece of white material turned into a dirty, dark-red colour. The darning was also a dismal failure.

It was obvious that Miss paid no heed to the Master. She was the boss. If the Master asked her to perform a certain duty, she would reply peevishly, 'I will do that in my own good time, Mr Jones.' And I remember once hearing her scream at him, 'Will you please mind your own business, Mr Jones.'

That made him retreat like a dog with its tail between its legs. It was a great shame that Miss Evans did not possess a little of her pluck and cheek.

I had been in Miss Evans's class for over a month, and all of a sudden she wasn't there – she was gone. The Master ordered us to take out our reading books, and to remain quiet. No explanation of any kind. But as always, Wili Weirglodd knew the answers.

'She is at home crying, because her sweetheart has been killed in France.'

And indeed, after a few days' absence, she appeared looking pale and wan, with a black band sewn to the sleeve of her blouse.

Eitel had been missing for over a week, and Wili Weirglodd knew the reason for that too. Apparently, Lloyd George had sent a policeman at dead of night to his house and had taken both Eitel and his mother to Swansea gaol. His mother was a Welsh woman, a local woman, married to a German, and her husband had been imprisoned when war first broke out. According to Wili, the Germans were responsible for the fighting and the killing of innocent people, and prison was too good a place for them. They should all be killed off. That was the only way to end the war. Poor Eitel! He was so harmless – too timid almost to move from his corner.

The war and its consequences worried everybody, and it was said that but for our own brave soldiers, the Germans would invade our country, and kill all our children, just as Herod had once slaughtered the children of Bethlehem.

I would run home from school every day, frightened, for fear that there was a German, lurking behind the hedgerows. I was even more terrified of the Germans than I was of the Master.

Everyone grumbled about the rations – no sugar, no tea, no butter. All the local farmers sent their butter and eggs to market in order to 'win the war', and if you did not have a cow, you had neither butter nor milk. We were alright; Marged would arrive every week laden with good food – nor did Auntie Mary arrive empty-handed.

Mamo had been so relaxed and happy throughout the summer, but suddenly, towards the beginning of autumn, her mood changed completely. She spent most of the day in bed and tea was never ready when I came home from school. Auntie Mary would call regularly but not even she could raise her from her misery. Marged had a fancy name for her illness. She called it 'melancholia'. I had never heard of it, and had no idea what it meant.

'What's wrong, Mamo?'

'Leave me alone, and go out to play.'

'Are you ill, Mamo?'

'It is worse than any illness – get out of my sight, for goodness' sake.'

And out I would go – down to Glan-dŵr to eat bread-and-butter with sugar spread on it. They always had sugar to spare for me.

'I'm worried about Mamo, Mari. She spends most of her time in bed. Marged calls it melancholia. What is "melancholia", Mari?'

'Melancholia is a great worry. Worrying about yourself, until you feel it is better to die than to live.'

'Is Mamo going to die, Mari?'

'No, no, of course not; she will be fine when your father returns.'

'And when will that be?'

'When the war ends.'

'The Germans are killing off our boys like

flies, and we shall never see any of them again. That's what Tomos y Gof says.'

Don't you listen to Tomos, he is a Judas. Lloyd George says that every soldier will be home for Christmas. He knows best, and he never lies.'

'Tomos y Gof says that Lloyd George is completely off his head, because he believes that the only way to win the war is to kill off every German. Every Jack-one.'

'That is what war is all about, Jini. Shooting and killing is the only way to win a war. And the more soldiers that are killed, the sooner the war will come to an end, and the country that kills most will win the war. It is as simple as that.'

'I don't believe we shall ever see Dyta again. Must we have a war, Mari? Do they have to kill one another?'

'Jini *fach*, you don't understand. But for our boys going overseas to fight, the Germans would have landed here, and killed us all off – men, women, children, babies, and all the animals too.'

'Why do the Germans want to come here?'

'Greed and revenge. You are too young to understand, Jini.'

'Do you understand, Mari?'

'I understand more than Tomos y Gof does. Never listen to him. What is more, he is a Conshie.'

I wanted to ask what 'conshie' meant, but I had learnt from experience when to stop asking awkward questions.

So off I went to play cards with Sara. Mari never joined in. She called them 'Satan's playthings'.

But I did not enjoy myself. I kept thinking of Dyta, far away in France, killing the Germans, and the Germans doing their best to kill him.

When I arrived home, Mamo was still in bed with her face turned towards the wall.

'Are you in pain, Mamo?'

'Jini, don't worry me. Boil yourself an egg, drink a cupful of milk, and go to bed.'

I could not eat anything, even though I had a big hole in my stomach. I went to bed quietly, fully believing that 'melancholia' was catching, just like the flu, and that I had caught the sickness from Mamo.

10

Not a word from Dyta, and Mamo spending the greater part of the day in bed. I prepared sandwiches for myself every morning – bread-and-butter, a piece of cheese, and a bottle of milk. Most of the children had only plain bread to eat; the farm children had butter and something extra on their bread. But Marged would visit us regularly with her basket laden with food; I never enquired who actually provided us with all those extras.

We were not supervised during the dinner hour, and the children who had no sort of filling in their bread would try to toast it on the open fire with the result that it burnt and tasted of smoke and coal. They would then pinch food from the children who were better fed, and it was often hell let loose in the 'babies' class. Miss always vanished during feeding time.

We all stank of camphor, because we carried a quantity of the small white balls in our pockets or stitched on to our clothes. Their purpose was to protect us from the flu. That was a terrible sickness, and people died like flies. Three children from one family died in the same week. Mari said that the flu was far more dangerous than the Germans. Miss and the

Master were away at the same time, and Miss Evans had to cope with the few children who were well enough to attend. We had a lovely time: singing, reciting, and play acting the stories she read to us. We sang Welsh hymns and English songs such as,

> Some speak of Alexander
> And some of Hercules,
> Of Hector and Lysander
> And such great names as these.
> But of all the world's great heroes
> There are none that can compare
> With a tow row, row, row, row, row
> To the British Grenadiers.

We had no idea who 'the great heroes' were, but we sang 'tow, row, row' with gusto, with shout and joy, not caring who they were.

School was a real pleasure when both the Master and Miss were laid up with the flu. She taught us to sing 'Hen Wlad Fy Nhadau' and not 'God Save the King' as the Master did.

Miss Evans had a beautiful singing voice. She had won prizes at local *eisteddfodau*, but she was not allowed to teach us music of any description, because according to the Master, 'the noise created a disturbance'.

But life at home was misery. Mamo stayed in bed, day after day after day.

Auntie Mary was down with the flu, and Marged 'was in bed, full of sickness' according to the man on horseback, who brought us a basketful of food every Friday. I had no idea who this stranger was, and his greeting was always the same.

'The boss sends you these goods; he wants the basket back.'

That was all, and on enquiring about Marged, his answer was always the same – 'she is full of sickness'.

Sara was also in bed, and Mari dosed her with some black treacly stuff, which she called 'black Jack', and bathed her feet in a mixture of mustard and hot brimstone. You could smell the stench half a mile away. I kept my distance, in case I would be handed out the same treatment. Mari had great faith in her own medicines, and if anyone questioned their efficiency, she always had a ready answer.

'Dr Powell always asks me for advice when his own medicines are a failure.'

No one dared disagree with Mari.

But her great worry was that she could not find a cure for consumption (tuberculosis), and she experimented continuously with various herbs. Consumption was a dreadful disease, and once you caught that, it was certain death. Men, women and children of all ages suffered from it. Jane Tŷ-draw died of it.

She was my friend; we were in the same class in school. She was spitting and coughing for months before her death, but no one dared utter the word 'consumption'. She was absent for about a week and then we received the terrible news that she had 'passed away'. People did not 'die' where we lived, they 'passed away'. They spoke of her sickness and death in a whisper, exactly as if it was her fault for having caught the sickness. Poor, dear Jane.

The Master and the children in her class attended the funeral. We all carried a flower to throw on the coffin. We all wept, even the boys, and some of us wailed aloud. Poor Jane's mother knelt down at the graveside and shouted, 'Jane, Jane, don't leave me. Come back, Jane dear.' Nobody listened to her. It was a dreadful feeling to hear the earth falling on the coffin, and to watch Jane's mother, screaming and sobbing, being dragged away from the graveside. Jane was her only child. Her husband was away in the army, and they had not seen him, neither had they heard from him for over a year. Jane was a bright, healthy girl when he had last seen her.

My mind was in a turmoil. I did not know whom or what to believe. The preacher said that Jane was now safe in the arms of Jesus. How could she possibly fly to heaven when she was enclosed in a wooden box, and buried deep down in the earth?

As soon as I arrived home I ran down to Glan-dŵr to try and find an answer to my doubts.

'Where has Jane gone to, Sara?'

'It was her body that was buried in the ground. Her soul has flown to heaven to Jesus Christ.'

'The soul? What is that, Sara?'

'The soul lives inside us, out of sight, hidden from the world. The soul does not die, and it is the soul that goes to heaven to live with Jesus Christ for ever and ever – Amen.'

'But Jesus Christ flew to heaven in a white robe; he also had a pair of wings to assist him. I saw his picture in your big Bible, Sara.'

'That is only a picture, Jini – every picture is not always accurate.'

'So everything you see and read in the Bible is not always true.'

'You ask too many questions for your own good, Jini. Come and play snakes-and-ladders.'

That was Sara's way of getting out of a tight corner. She thought that by playing a silly game I would have forgotten all about death and the soul. But she was wrong. I would ask Mari again at the right moment. She was wiser, and seemed to understand the Bible far better than Sara. It would have been useless to ask Mamo. She spent day after day with her face turned to the wall, and was quite determined not to call the doctor. Melancholia is a fearful disease. I felt miserable.

Life at school was also a misery. The Master was back, but not Miss. So Miss Evans had to teach the 'babies', and Standards II and III had to move up to the Master's class.

In Miss Evans's class we were allowed to write in copy books using lead pencils, but the Master gave us slates and stone pencils with which to write, just as we did with Miss. We were forever writing the same sentence over and over again, spitting on it, rubbing everything out, starting all over again, and on and on, non-stop. And to crown it all, the Master asked John Pensarn, a real duffer, to listen to our spelling-out and reading. We had to be as quiet as mice, or the Master would attack us like a wild bull, roaring and punching us with his bare fists until our backs and arms were covered with bruises. He was a cruel old man.

I showed my bruises to Mamo; she grudgingly turned her face from the wall to look at them. She was surprised and shocked, and said in a trembling voice, 'You need not go to school tomorrow, Jini – you may stay at home.'

Thank goodness. So off I went to Glan-dŵr to show off my bruises, and to repeat what everybody said, 'The Master is a cruel old man'.

But Mari, as always, was ready with her words of wisdom.

'Don't blame him; he is taking revenge on anybody and everybody, because the Germans killed his only child.'

I was fed and cosseted at Glan-dŵr. We read the *Tivy-side* together, and were amazed that there was not one story or a happy incident in the paper from beginning to end, only reports of funerals, and a long list of soldiers who were either missing or killed in action. I read the list carefully, but Dyta's name was not included, thank goodness. I hated the war, and wished with all my heart that it would come to an end quickly.

11

At long last the war came to an abrupt end. Nothing lasts for ever, apart from the Holy Gospel, according to Mari. We realised it was over when we heard the train whistling non-stop in the far distance, and when Sara and Mari ran towards our house bubbling over with excitement, shouting, 'Peace, peace for evermore.' They ran from house to house, proclaiming the good tidings, hoping that they would be the first to carry the news.

At first we could hardly believe it. I was born a few months before war broke out. I could remember nothing else. I had no idea what life was like in time of peace. During my short life it had always been war, fighting, killing, sorrow, rations and vague promises.

'You shall have a kitten when the war ends.'

'You shall have a new frock.'

'You shall have a new story-book.'

'You shall have a new doll.'

But when the war did end, I had nothing – 'not a bloody thing', as Dyta would have said.

Neither did Dyta come home, but we received a very important letter stamped with the letter O.H.M.S. soon afterwards.

When I arrived home from school the letter remained unopened on the table.

'Open it, Jini,' said Mamo.

I was afraid to open it. A letter stamped with O.H.M.S. was the way Lloyd George chose to inform people that a relative had been killed. So said Mari, but Mari was not always right.

I opened it cautiously with Mamo peeping over my shoulder. The words danced before my eyes, 'Wounded in action', and it went on to say that he was a patient in a hospital, somewhere in England. I was so relieved, but Mamo said nothing. She pursed her lips, and went back to bed.

We all celebrated the great peace. No more war. This was a war to end all wars. The boys who were killed were forgotten. No school, and the train continued to whistle daily. There were fun and games, singing and dancing everywhere. The land-girls downed their tools, and rushed back to wherever they had come from. The land-girl who worked at Rhyd heard the good news when she was halfway through milking a cow. She left the bucket just where it was under the cow, and ran to catch the first train home, leaving Daniel Jones the farmer flabbergasted.

I was allowed to attend a 'celebration concert' at school in the company of Sara and Mari. It was a concert where everybody sang and shouted. We sang with gusto hymns like 'Calon Lân', and also 'It's a long way to Tipperary'. It did not matter whether or not we knew the words, the main purpose was to create a noise and have fun. We drank tea, without sugar, and coloured water which they called lemonade, ate sandwiches and yellow cake. I did enjoy myself.

Then amidst all the fun, the Rector stood up, raised his hand and in a voice of authority called, 'Silence'. We all obeyed. He asked us all to stand quietly, and to remember the brave boys who had died so that we could live in peace – the brave boys who would never again return to their native land.

That was the end of the concert. We all went home in silence thinking of those brave boys, who had died to save our country from the Germans. I thought of Dyta. He too must have been near to death, or he would not have been wounded.

Some weeks later, on a Saturday afternoon, I was sitting quietly reading the *Tivy-side* – reading the account of the celebration concerts and the long list of the dead and missing, when I heard a loud knock at the door. As usual, Mamo was in bed. It was a threatening knock.

'Who's there?'

'Open up, and you shall see.'

Dyta's voice, there was no mistaking it. I opened the door nervously. And there he was. Dyta himself. He looked pale and thin, minus the ruddy complexion and the pouch belly, and leaning on crutches. But he was Dyta all right. A man in uniform (not a khaki uniform) stood by him, and when he saw that the door had opened, he said bluntly, 'Goodbye, Private John, and good luck.'

And he was gone.

Dyta was back, and I just stared at him in awe, not knowing what to say, not knowing what to do.

'Jini, *cariad*, it's me. Don't you recognise your Dyta? Have you nothing to say?'

No, I had nothing to say. I tried to appear pleased, but it was difficult. I *should* have been pleased, but I did not fancy the look of that man. He spoke quietly in a hoarse voice. Dyta was not like that.

'Where's your mother?'

'Mamo is ill, very ill – she has been ill for weeks.'

Then Mamo appeared on the scene, dressed in a long white nightgown; her long shining hair falling in waves over her shoulders, and her big blue eyes glistening from surprise and shock. She looked just like Delilah, whose picture I had seen in the big Bible, but much more beautiful. Dyta started at her in amazement. Neither spoke. The silence was painful.

Then Dyta blurted out, 'You have swallowed a bloody frog. When? Tell me.'

'In about two months' time.'

Tears rolled down her cheeks, and she made no effort to control herself.

Dyta then lifted both his hands, and counted his fingers slowly, one by one, just as Miss used to teach us sums in the 'babies'.

'Good Lord – hell's bells.'

Silence – dead silence, which spoke louder than words. Neither moved – they stared at each other like two cockerels raring for a fight.

I was frightened, I could not understand their silly talk. So I sneaked out of the house and ran to Glan-dŵr; perhaps they could enlighten me.

'Sara, have you ever swallowed a frog?'

'You are talking nonsense, Jini.'

'Dyta asked Mamo if she had swallowed a frog. What did he mean?'

'Has your father come home? Surprise, surprise.'

They must have known he had arrived, because they could see everybody and everything that passed their house. To avoid answering, they started asking *me* questions.

'How is he?'

'Is he able to walk?'

'Is he badly wounded?'

'What a surprise.'

And on and on non-stop, just to avoid answering my question. But I persisted.

'Sara, answer my question. What did Dyta mean when he asked Mamo if she had swallowed a frog?'

They both looked sheepishly at each other; then Mari cleared her throat and said in a know-all voice, 'Your father has just returned from France, and I understand that the French eat frogs for breakfast.'

I knew full well that they were shirking from telling me the truth, and I knew too, that it would be quite useless to carry on asking.

So I went home, low in mind and spirit. Mamo had gone to bed, and Dyta was finishing his supper – fried ham and eggs as usual.

'Are you glad to see me, Jini, *cariad*?'

'Yes, Dyta.'

He then embraced me and kissed me wildly – his hand creeping under my dress, trying to get at my cuckoo. I was embarrassed, I felt sick, and as soon as I was able to free myself, I climbed the ladder into the loft, and into bed, out of his sight. There was no end to his fondling, his kissing and his groping. I wished Mamo was half as loving as he was. I did not sleep, I kept worrying about the frog that Mamo had swallowed.

The following day he spent his time cleaning, oiling, and pumping the tyres of his rickety old bike, and by tea time he was away on his iron horse with his crutches tied to the bar. That was the pattern of all his days from that time onwards – off in the morning on his bike after breakfast, back late at night to fry himself ham and eggs, and then to bed.

Mamo stayed in her bed all day and every day, and I had to fend for myself, but after school I spent most of my time at Glan-dŵr. What would I have done without Sara and Mari?

One night I had a horrific experience. It must have been around midnight when I heard Dyta climbing the ladder into my bedroom. Why? There was no room for anyone else in my bed.

I heard him stripping off his clothes, and before I realised it, he was pulling off my nightdress – no, not pulling, but tearing it away. He embraced me savagely, and threw himself on top of me.

'Don't Dyta, you're suffocating me, you're killing me.'

'Shut your gob, you little devil,' and placed his hand over my mouth. I tried to struggle, but he squeezed and pushed – pushed something hard into my body. I was in pain. I could not scream. He kept my head down under the blanket. But I made a mighty struggle, and somehow I managed to lift my head out of the blanket. I bit his hand, and yelled with all the strength that was left in me.

'Mamo, Mamo. Help, help. Dyta is trying to kill me.'

Then I heard Mamo's voice calling from the bottom of the stairs.

'Jini, come down, at once.'

Dyta tried to stop me, but by this time I was hysterical and I believe Mamo's stern voice brought him to his senses too. I freed myself, flew down the ladder and ran stark naked into Mamo's arms.

I felt sick, and my lower body was smarting painfully. I could not control my sobs and hiccups. Neither could Mamo – we both wept throughout the long, long night.

In the morning I was surprised to find that Mamo had got up early, and had prepared my breakfast. I could not eat anything; my only thought was to run away from Dyta – away as far as possible. Mamo prepared my dinner sandwiches and said, 'Jini, I beg of you not to tell anyone of what happened last night. Do you hear me? Not one word. That must be kept a secret. Sara and Mari must not be told. Promise me, Jini, and I promise you, in the name of God, that never will you have to suffer that sort of torment ever again.'

'I promise, Mamo.'

She kissed me, and I felt a lot better. There was no need for her to ask me not to tell. I was so ashamed of what had happened – ashamed of myself, and ashamed of Dyta too for acting like a beast.

I must have looked a sorry sight when I arrived in school, because Miss Evans stared at me in a pitiful way and said, 'Jini, what's wrong? Do you feel all right?'

'I am fine, thank you, Miss.'

'What is that bruise on your neck, Jini? May I have a look.'

'No, I'm all right Miss, indeed Miss.'

'Jini, the truth. How did it happen?'

'Please Miss, I want to go to the "go-out".'

I ran to the 'go-out' – I sat on the seat, and cried and cried. It was painful to pass water, and there was a scorching fire inside me. I could not possibly return to the class to face Miss Evans, and tell her more lies, so I entered the porch quietly, grabbed my bag and coat and ran without looking backwards, towards home.

I would not be able to call at Glan-dŵr, because they would surely ask me why I would be running home at that time of day. And I am certain they would notice my bruises, and I did not want anybody, not a living person, to find out what had happened in our house on that dreadful night. So I took the path along the riverside, and sat exhausted on the bank. I took off my boots and stockings and washed my feet. I then took my handkerchief and bathed my bruises in the cold water. I felt damaged all over. I also felt sick, but I could not vomit – it remained as a hard lump in my stomach. I also washed my lower parts, very gently – the pain was almost unbearable.

I threw my sandwiches to the fish, and sat on the river bank with my feet in the water for a long, long time. Then I heard the herd boy from Pen-banc calling '*trw fach, trw fach*' – calling the cows home to be milked. I knew then, that it would be around three o'clock, so I decided to venture home, hoping that Dyta would have disappeared out of my sight, out of my life.

'You are very early, Jini,' said Mamo. Surprise, surprise, she was not in bed.

'Yes, Mamo,' and I started to weep.

'Oh, Jini *fach*, you have been badly hurt.'

Her voice was gentler and more sympathetic than I had ever heard her, and that made me cry all the more. She caught hold of me and embraced me tenderly, and that was the first time in my entire life that Mamo had given me a really close cuddle, a real *cwtsh*. I felt so much better for it. I loved my Mamo.

'Where is Dyta?'

'He has gone away – to Pembrokeshire, I believe. Don't worry, Jini – he won't return in a hurry. Listen, I want you to understand this. He will not abuse you like that ever again; not as long as I am here to protect you.'

'Are you sure, Mamo?'

She hugged me again, and we both wept. For the first time ever, I felt we both understood each other, and that in spite of the pain, the bruises and the shame, I felt happier than I had ever been.

We had pancakes for tea, and I told her the whole story of how I had run away from school, of the pain and the shame, and how I had washed myself in the stream.

'Jini, you must go to bed early tonight, and you need not go to school tomorrow.'

At bedtime I started to climb the steps to the loft as usual.

'No, Jini. From now on you will sleep downstairs in my bed. Your father will sleep in the attic.'

About seven o'clock there was a knock at the door. Panic! I prayed. 'Please, dear Jesus – not Dyta, please. Keep him away from me.'

And indeed, Jesus heard me and obeyed. It was Miss Evans. She had never been to our house before, and Mamo had no idea who she was. I heard her say, 'I am Jini's teacher, and I am worried about her. She ran away from school this morning without telling anybody. Is she ill?'

'She's better now,' Mamo said sharply. 'She fell down the stairs last night and bruised herself, that's all.'

Neither spoke for a short time. Then Miss Evans said, 'I am sorry, I was worried.'

'There is no need to worry – Jini is fine. I did not catch your name?'

'Miss Evans – Jini's teacher.'

'Thank you for your concern, Miss Evans. Jini will be back in school next week. Goodnight.'

I thought Mamo had been rather curt and discourteous. But really Mamo was ashamed – ashamed of herself, and ashamed that she was married to a man who was a beast and a bully, and that same bully had abused her little girl brutally and unforgivably.

12

A week passed – a whole week with only Mamo and myself at home. We did not see or hear from Dyta – neither was he missed. I stayed away from Glan-dŵr, in case I would be asked awkward questions about my absence from school, and I would have to lie. Marged arrived as usual, complete with basket. Auntie Mary also came, looking sad, and on the verge of tears. She filled the big brass pan with warm soapy water, and bathed me gently. She also rubbed some soothing ointment on my legs and thighs. I had more bruises on my body than I had on my neck and chest. She kissed and embraced me lovingly and said, 'Jini, try to forget the dreadful thing that has happened to you. It will never happen to you again. Your mother will see to that.'

But easier said than done. I would wake up wildly at dead of night and scream hysterically, 'Dyta, don't, don't. You're hurting me.'

Mamo would then take me in her arms, cuddle me, and say, 'There, there, all is well now, *cariad*.'

But one blessing arose out of all the nasty business. I realised that Mamo loved me dearly. I heard her and Auntie Mary talking quietly when they thought I was asleep.

'What will you do when Ifan returns? But maybe he has gone for good.'

'Oh no, Mary, he will return. I am certain of that. He knows full well which side of the bread is buttered.'

'What can you do, Myfi, in your present condition?'

'Don't you worry, Mary. From now on, I shall be boss, and Ifan John will have to learn to obey. He will be lucky if he will be allowed a mattress to sleep on, in the loft.'

'I suppose you know best, Myfi. But if I were you I would seek the advice of a solicitor.'

'No Mary, I shall settle this business in my own way. But I want you to promise faithfully that you will not utter one word about this to anybody – not a whisper. Promise?'

'Of course – I promise. But what about Jini?'

'Jini is old and wise enough to keep a secret. The shame and the disgrace have sunk more deeply than the bruises.'

There was silence for a short time, and suddenly Auntie Mary said with conviction in her voice, 'The devil should be castrated.'

And I quietly added 'Amen' to that.

The following week, I attended school. They all wanted to know why I had been absent. I learnt to lie easily. 'I hurt my back, falling down the attic steps.'

But I could not fool Miss Evans. She was

extremely concerned, and wanted to examine my bruises.

'Did you visit the doctor, Jini?'

'No, but Auntie Mary rubbed some ointment on my back.'

'You need not go out to play, Jini – you may stay in the classroom. I will give you a book to read.'

I stayed inside for a whole week with Miss Evans as company. I was so grateful, because my body still ached, and my legs were too stiff to run around the playground.

A fortnight passed, and Dyta still had not returned home. Mamo made certain to bolt the door before going to sleep. But one night as we were having supper, there was a loud knock at the door, and a fumbling of the latch. Dyta! There was another knock, and another. I was terrified. Mamo was quite calm, she took her time, and opened the door slowly. And there was Dyta, the full six feet of him, looking dirty and unshaven. He did not even glance at us, and walked into the bedroom.

'Ifan,' said Mamo sharply, 'out of there. The attic is your sleeping quarters from now on.'

He obeyed sheepishly without uttering a word, and slowly climbed the ladder. And from that moment onwards, that was the pattern of life in our home. I hardly ever saw him. He used to leave for work early every morning, never returned for supper, and when he did return, very late at night, he would climb the stairs, hobbling and shuffling his way up noisily.

But I worried – Mamo was ill, very ill, all day and every day. Even during the dark hours in bed at night, she would toss and turn, sigh and sob. That would wake me up. I could not bear to hear her groan. But one night the groan turned into a cry, a horrible, long, drawn-out cry. I was terrified and had no idea what to do. But fortunately Dyta heard it also, he limped down the steps, and ventured into our room.

'Ifan,' Mamo screamed, 'run, fetch Mary – run at once – there is no time to lose.'

He was still lame, but he could ride his bike, and off he went obediently, without muttering a word.

I got up. I dressed quickly, but had not the vaguest idea of what to do. But Mamo began to give me instructions.

'Jini, poke the embers, get the fire going. Fill the big kettle – we shall need boiling water.'

But she continued to wail and moan, getting out of bed, getting back to bed, throwing away the bedclothes, and telling me to open the window. 'I am suffocating, Jini.'

Oh God, it was terrible. I was frightened. Was she going to die?

'Mamo, Mamo, please don't die. I love you.'

I thought a prayer might help.

'Please, Jesus Christ, don't let Mamo die. I promise to be a good girl all the days of my life, if only you will keep Mamo alive.'

I could do nothing more – the kettle was already boiling, so I continued to pray.

Then I heard the sound of a horse's hooves outside on the gravel. Thank God, Auntie Mary had arrived, and she took over. Dyta soon followed.

'Ifan, fetch the doctor – at once – there is no time to lose. Hurry man! And Jini, you run to Glan-dŵr and ask Mari to come up. She has acted as a midwife before – she knows what to do in an emergency. Run, child.'

I ran and I ran – they were both in bed, asleep. I knocked frantically at their bedroom window.

'Mari, come at once, Mamo is dying.'

Mari dressed hastily, opened the door and said, 'Calm down, Jini *fach*, your mother is not going to die. You stay here with Sara.'

I stayed, reluctantly.

'Sara, what is a midwife?'

'It is the name given to the woman who helps the mother when a baby is born.'

'Baby? Who is going to have a baby?'

'Your mother, Jini *fach*.'

'Mamo? Is that why she is so ill?'

'Yes Jini, *cariad*.'

'So Mamo is not going to die?'

'Of course not – she is going to have a baby, that's all.'

'I don't understand.'

'Did she not tell you?'

'No. Where do babies come from?'

'The baby grows inside the mother for a long time – nine months to be exact.'

'Who put it inside her in the first place?'

'Your father, of course. But listen, Jini, it is not my place to explain these things to you. You must ask your mother. What about a cup of tea and a game of snakes-and-ladders?'

Typical of Sara – that was how she solved every awkward question. So we drank tea and played snakes-and-ladders for hours, until I felt like a big snake myself, climbing up to a point, and no further. I was dead tired, worried about Mamo, and trying to work out how and when did Dyta succeed in planting a baby inside her.

'You had better sleep here tonight, Jini.'

'Why?'

'You are tired, darling. You shall sleep in our bed until Mari arrives.'

'I want to go home, Sara. I want to see the baby.'

'There won't be a baby until tomorrow. You shall go home when Mari returns.'

I put on Sara's nightgown and went to bed. But I did not sleep. I kept hearing Mamo's screams with her face so red and swollen. Giving birth to a baby is a dreadful sickness, worse than the flu. Must the mother suffer such agony? I made up my mind, there and then, that I would never, never have a baby – no, not ever.

After a long, long time, I heard the door open. The dawn was breaking. Mari! I ran to meet her.

'Mari, has the baby arrived?'

'Yes, a little boy.'

'I am going home.'

'Jini, listen to me,' she said very quietly, 'you had better stay here for a while longer.'

'Why?'

'Your mother needs to rest.'

'How is she?' asked Sara.

'We were fortunate that Dr Powell arrived when he did.'

Sara and Mari looked at each other and spoke with their eyes. I knew then that all was not well. They placed a mattress on the floor by the big bed and brought out a blanket from the cupboard.

'Come, Jini *fach*, lie down for a short while, and try to sleep. Is is far too early to get up, and we are all exhausted.'

'I want to go home, Mari. I want to see the baby.'

'Your mother needs peace and quiet. She has been so ill.'

'Is she in pain? Has she stopped screaming?'

'Yes dear, she is much better, but is weak and weary and does not want to be disturbed.'

Strangely, once I put my head on the pillow, I slept like a log, and it was twelve o'clock before I woke up. Sara's *cawl* was a real treat, and I ate my fill, before I ran home.

Auntie Mary was still there, looking very tired. So was Marged. There was no sign of Dyta, and Marged was in charge.

'Hush, not one word, not a sound, your mother is fast asleep.'

'I want to see the baby, Marged.'

'Follow me, quietly – not a whisper.'

Mamo was sleeping peacefully. She looked so pale and so beautiful with her long black tresses framing her face. And there on a chair by her side, in the drawer of the chiffonier, was the little baby – my brother. I was so disappointed. He was so tiny, such a weakling, and his face was as yellow as a dandelion. But he had a good crop of hair; bright ginger, just like Dyta's. I was not allowed to touch him.

'Out you go now. We are expecting the Rector any minute.'

'The Rector? What does he want here?'

'He is going to baptise the baby.'

'Baptise? He's too tiny to be baptised. He won't understand.'

'No baby understands, but the Rector does. Every child must have a name.'

'And what will his name be, Marged?'

'Your mother has already named him.'

'Yes? What is it?'

'David Lloyd – David Lloyd John, of course.'

'What a big name for such a weakling. Was I baptised, Marged?'

'Yes, when you were six months old.'

'Why the hurry to baptise the baby, Marged?'

Marged paused to think, and then spoke slowly in her Sunday-best voice.

'You might as well know. The little baby is ill, very ill indeed, and he might not live for six months. But if he is baptised he will die a Christian, and then they will have the right to bury him the graveyard where all Christians are buried. Otherwise he would be buried in a far corner of the churchyard, where all the heathens, and those who have not been baptised are buried.'

'Will the Rector be able to turn the baby into a Christian, Marged?'

At that the Rector arrived, and Marged uttered a sigh of relief. I believe she was glad that she was not obliged to answer any more of my awkward questions. I knew the Rector. He used to call sometimes to see Mamo, but he would never enter the house. He was always in a hurry.

We all gathered together by Mamo's bed. She tried to sit up, but she was too weak to stand the strain. Auntie Mary held the baby in her arms. He was dressed in a most beautiful lace shawl, and mewing like a kitten. Marged was fussing around, carrying water in a silver bowl – a bowl which I had never before seen.

She placed it reverently on the table beside the bed.

To my surprise Dyta appeared from nowhere, shaven and dressed in his walking-out suit with a collar and tie.

The Rector took hold of the baby, who was still mewing, turned to Mamo and asked, 'What is the baby's name, Mrs John?'

'David Lloyd.'

'Hold on,' said Dyta. 'I want to give him my father's name instead of that Lloyd. Lloyd is the name of the *crachach*, the snobs.'

'And what is your father's name, Mr John?'

'A good old Welsh name – Joshua.'

The Rector smiled, and turned to Mamo.

'The name of Lloyd is to remain,' she said. 'You may push in the other name, if you wish.'

And so the baby was christened David Joshua Lloyd. Water was sprinkled on his forehead from the silver bowl, and he was baptised in the name of the Father, the Son, and the Holy Ghost. I had no idea who they were, but David Joshua Lloyd John was now worthy to be buried in the same place as all Christians, and not in the top, far corner of the churchyard that was reserved for those who had never been baptised.

David Joshua Lloyd John was divested of his beautiful lace shawl, and was gently returned to the chiffonier drawer.

According to Marged he slept soundly and quietly that night, for the first time since his birth.

13

Life at Llety'r Wennol was never the same again. He only weighed four and a half pounds, but the care and work entailed were a tremendous weight on Marged's old shoulders. Mamo remained ill and feeble, and spent most of her time in bed. Dyta tended to loiter around, until Marged told him bluntly, 'Go – and get out of my sight.'

'Go to where?'

'Go to wherever you came from. But stay away from me. Go to shovel air.'

And he obeyed like a lamb! Marged was the boss, and she appeared to enjoy her new role in life. Mari would arrive every morning to bathe and dress David Joshua Lloyd. Mamo was adamant about the baby's name. He was to be called David, pronounced in the English way and not 'Dai, Davy or Dafydd'. When Mamo was not around, Dyta would address him as 'Joshua' – 'out of respect for the old man, God bless his soul.'

I had to go to Glan-dŵr every night to sleep – on the mattress on the floor. I was glad to escape from the baby's whimpering. Marged slept alongside Mamo in the big bed, and it was Marged who got up at all hours to attend to the baby's needs.

He never stopped whining, never cried aloud, and remained as yellow as a new sovereign.

A man on horseback called daily with a basketful of food, and Marged saw that some of it was sent to Glan-dŵr. According to Marged, 'it costs to raise children'. I was the 'children'. I had all my meals at Glan-dŵr, and they were good.

Mamo spent most of her time in bed, gazing at the wall. She had no desire to get up, no desire to eat, and refused to breast-feed the baby. Marged did her best to bottle-feed him with a mixture of milk, sugar and water, but he retched most of it. Poor Marged, poor baby, and above all, poor Mamo.

But one day Dr Powell arrived. No one was expecting him, least of all Mamo. He took one look at the baby, shook his head and said nothing. He turned to Mamo and said sharply, 'Myfanwy, this won't do. You must get up, and attend to the baby yourself – breast-feed him. The child needs a mother's care. Marged is getting on in years, and all the extra work you place on her is too much for her at her age. I know that you are weak and low-spirited but the longer you stay in bed, the weaker you will become. Come on my girl. Shift.'

Then Mamo started to cry, loud and long. Dr Powell held her hand lovingly without saying one word, and allowed her to sob to the depths of her soul.

At long last he said, 'There, there, Myfanwy, don't lock up your innermost thoughts – always share them, and always remember your ancestry. You are one of the Lloyds – no one can deprive you of that honour.'

When I arrived home from school the following day, I found Mamo up and dressed, and nursing little David by the fireside. It was good to see them both together.

But one day, soon afterwards, as I entered the gate I saw Dr Powell's trap and pony. I knew instinctively that something was wrong. Mamo? Oh no, please Jesus Christ, not Mamo.'

It was the baby. There he was, the tiny weakling lying in Marged's lap. The whimpering had ceased, but his eyes were wide open, and a strange feeling possessed me; this frail creature was my brother, a close relation, someone who would one day grow to help me, and someone I could love and respect. And he was dying. Otherwise Dr Powell would not be here. It was rumoured that Dr Powell only attended a sick person when he was on the verge of death. The poor had not the money to pay the doctor for unnecessary visits. Yet, it was also said that Dr Powell himself was a poor man, because he never bothered to send out bills to those who could not afford to pay.

I looked at my little brother closely, and saw him properly for the first time – big blue eyes, a thick cover of red hair, his arms and face were of a yellowish colour. His eyes were wide open, as if staring into the unknown, and yet not able to see anything. He uttered not a sound, not a moan.

'May I touch him, Marged?'

'Yes dear, but gently, very gently.'

That was the first time I came into contact with my brother, and I felt a sharp sensation running through my body.

'May I kiss him, Marged?'

Marged looked at Mamo, and she nodded. They all stood around like dumb animals. I bent down and kissed him on the cheek. I am certain that he smiled; then the big blue eyes closed. Dr Powell placed his hand on his chest, and held it there for some time. Then he turned to Mamo and said, 'It is all over, Myfanwy – I can do no more.'

We all knew what he meant. He shook hands with Mamo and left. The puny thing was only three weeks and five days old. I hardly knew him, but I felt that I had lost someone who was very close and precious to me. I wanted to weep, but the tears refused to come. Mamo lifted David, she kissed and caressed him – caressing a dead baby. Perhaps she too felt the loss; she nearly lost her life giving birth to him.

Marged tried to console her through her tears, 'Don't worry, Miss Myfanwy, he shall have a funeral worthy of his family.'

Then I remembered the christening. David Joshua Lloyd John would be buried, not in the far corner of the churchyard, but in the family grave in the part where all Christians are buried.

Marged was now in charge.

'Jini *fach*, you had better go down to Glan-dŵr to stay for a few days. We shall be very busy here preparing for the funeral. You will not be expected to attend school next week, because your little brother has passed away.'

According to Marged, he was not dead – he had just 'passed away'.

And to Glan-dŵr I went. I felt so miserable – I did not feel like reading; I did not want to hear a story; I did not even want to talk. There was a lump in the pit of my stomach which prevented me from crying, and from laughing. Sara went on and on, without stop, relating tales about her as a child. She laughed at her own jokes, but nothing could persuade me to laugh, and the lump remained intact in my stomach.

There I remained until the day of the funeral. They both accompanied me back to the house that day to witness the ceremony of 'bidding farewell to the departed'.

Mamo sat by the fireside, dressed in black,

looking pale and distressed, but dry-eyed. Auntie Mary sat next to her and held her hand. Dyta hovered around, accompanied by a stranger. I realised later that he was his brother – my uncle. They both wore dark suits and black ties – deep mourning.

The Rector arrived. We all moved to the *pen-ucha* – the end room – Mamo's bedroom, to see David in his coffin – to see him for the last time. Mamo stooped down to kiss him. I did likewise. It was like kissing a stone. The lid of the coffin was screwed down noisily. The Rector then read from the English Bible that was kept hidden in a drawer in Mamo's bedroom. He read a chapter about Jesus Christ blessing little children and welcoming them to heaven. He then prayed for the baby's soul, and sympathised with my mother 'and the little girl'. There was no mention of Dyta.

Outside, the hearse, drawn by a big white horse stood waiting – a huge contraption for such a tiny coffin. Dyta and the stranger carried the coffin to the hearse. They both sat in front with the driver and off they went. Auntie Mary, Marged and Mari followed in a governess trap.

Marged wept profusely. I tried my best to produce tears, but I couldn't. The lump remained in my stomach and I felt sick. Mamo, I am certain, felt as I did.

Mamo and I stayed at home, and so did Sara, in order to prepare 'the funeral tea'.

I refused to go to the churchyard. I did not want to see my little brother being dropped into a black hole in the ground, and no one had been able to explain to me how anyone could arise from such a hole to live for ever with Jesus Christ.

Mamo was so quiet – she went back to sit by the fireside. Then, without warning, she embraced me tenderly and said, 'Thank the Good Lord, that I have you Jini, to love and to comfort me.'

And strangely the lump in my stomach eased considerably after Mamo said that.

14

Later they all returned from the funeral, ready to consume the funeral tea that Sara had prepared. Dyta followed half an hour or so later on his own; the stranger had disappeared. Sara and Mari left early, but Auntie Mary and Marged remained to comfort Mamo. No one took any notice of Dyta – until he entered the end-room to take off his funeral attire. Mamo followed him, and spoke angrily with venom in her voice.

'Ifan, take everything you own, out of this room, *now*. Take whatever you possess to the cockloft, and never enter this room again; not as long as you live. Understand?'

'You are a bloody hard woman, Fan.'

'At long last, I feel strong enough to stand up to your misbehaviour and lies. I am trying hard to preserve just a tiny part of my self-respect. You shall not tread on me and abuse me ever again, Ifan John. Get out.'

Never in my life had I heard Mamo speak in such a way. I was both shocked and glad at the same time. Auntie Mary and Marged listened to every word, and there was the shadow of a smirk hovering around their lips.

Dyta climbed up the ladder, like a puppy

that had had its tail docked. He came down in his walking-out suit, minus his collar and tie, and went out without saying one word, to find his comfort elsewhere. He was not wanted at Llety'r Wennol.

Auntie Mary departed soon afterwards, and Mamo accompanied her as far as the gate. She had not been outside the house for months. But, alas, Marged stayed. I was anxious to have Mamo to myself, just the two of us.

'When are you going home, Marged?'

'Tomorrow, *bach*, I shall stay tonight to keep your mother company.'

'But Marged, I shall be here.'

'Yes dear, only for tonight; it is a tradition that a relative stays with the bereaved for the first night, to comfort them in their *hiraeth*.'

'What about Dyta?'

'*Ych*,' was all she said, but it was a groan that arose from the depths of her soul.

'Is the baby safe in the arms of Jesus now, Marged?'

'Yes, of course. Jesus said quite clearly. "Suffer little children to come unto me".'

'Are you quite sure, Marged?'

'Yes, quite sure.'

'Why did they put him in a box and bury him? And why was he dressed in that beautiful white frock?'

'Your mother chose to dress him in that

frock. She was baptised in those clothes herself, and so were you. But if a baby dies it is the custom to bury him in his christening robe.'

'But David was not baptised in those clothes, Marged. He was wrapped in a shawl.'

'Dr Powell thought then that he had only a couple of hours to live, and there was no time to fetch the clothes.'

'And now he lies hidden in the earth in his beautiful frock. How is it possible for him to arise from that box and fly into the arms of Jesus?'

'It is not the body that rises to heaven, but the soul, the body remains in the ground until the resurrection.'

'And when will that be?'

'When the world comes to an end.'

'So dressing him in those beautiful clothes was sheer waste?'

Mamo returned, and that put an end to my questions. Mamo would tell me nothing – every time I asked her a question, she would shut up like a cockle shell and say, 'You are too young to understand, yet.'

But I learnt more than she realised by listening behind closed doors, and also by only pretending to sleep in my cockloft bed.

Auntie Mary and Mamo always spoke English to each other – posh English – not the same kind of English as the Master and

Miss spoke to us. Their English had a Welsh sound.

Marged returned home the following day. Someone came to fetch her in a trap and pony. I never found out where she lived, and neither did I find out the source of the food and all the other good things she used to bring along. Marged was a mystery.

Mamo never went shopping, she hardly ever went further than the end of the lane. Auntie Mary bought my clothes; Mamo never needed new clothes. The big wardrobe was bursting with lovely clothes – clothes she never wore.

One day, John Saer the carpenter paid us a visit. It was he who made David's coffin, and I could not forget the way he clamped down the lid, and the grinding of the screws echoing throughout the house. No, I did not like John Saer. He made certain that David would never be able to rise to heaven from that screwed-down casket. But Mamo was pleased to see him – that was a change; she did not welcome strangers as a rule.

'I understand you need a new bolt on the door, Mrs John. Very sensible too, with so many good-for-nothing tramps and unemployed soldiers prying around. Poverty, Mrs John, that is the reason for all the mischief and trouble that happens all around us today. It is a wicked world, Mrs John. Where are the good days that

Lloyd George promised us? I see no sign of them. All lies, all lies.'

He took out his tools, and started hammering the front door. The bolt on the front door worked perfectly.

'No, Mr Davies, stop, not that door. I need the bolt on the inside of the bedroom door – the end room.'

He raised his eyebrows, then nodded his head, as if he understood the situation, and carried on with his business.

He refused to accept payment.

'I was honoured to make the coffin for the baby, Mrs John. I hope it was to your liking.'

He doffed his cap, and away he went.

What a strange thing to say. It was only a tiny box with a lid, and its only purpose was to hold my dead brother out of sight, deep down in the ground. I was glad to see the last of John Saer.

'Why do you need a bolt on the bedroom door, Mamo?'

'Jini, you of all people should know. Have you forgotten how you were abused and ill-treated by your father?'

The truth dawned on me. I remembered the thumping and the clattering of the bed, Mamo's sobs, and the pain in her eyes the following morning. She too had suffered, but she suffered in silence. Poor, darling Mamo.

I ventured to ask, 'Did he abuse you too?'

She was silent for a few moments, as if she was trying to make her mind up what to say.

'Yes, Jini, but the situation was different. In my case the law was on his side, and I am afraid that I was to blame too. But all that is behind me now. He won't get another chance. That is why I needed a bolt on the door.'

I did not quite understand, but I understood enough. Enough to realise that Dyta was not a man to be trusted.

15

I was now in Standard III, and attending school was pure joy. We were taught all kinds of sums – we read stories about the English kings, and Miss Evans did her best to introduce us to Welsh history, without the help of any books on the subject.

The Master was absent a great deal, and that gave Miss Evans the chance to narrate stories about our own country – stories that described how the Welsh had suffered under English rule – the story of the 'Welsh not', and the 'Treason of the Blue Books'. We were amazed, and she impressed upon us that we should be proud of our own country, and never, never believe that the English were superior to us. But she had to be very careful. She had to be certain that both Miss and the Master were out of earshot, because neither liked to hear Welsh spoken in the classroom.

It seemed strange to me that the Master spoke Welsh to us outside school hours, and sometimes even during lessons. He would rant and rave and call us '*y diawled twp*' – 'you stupid devils'.

I was only eight, but I could do all sorts of sums – multiplication and long division. I could read English with ease, but there were no Welsh books available (apart from a few poetry books). But Miss Evans would present us with Welsh periodicals to take home to read.

When Mamo realised that I was fond of reading she said that there was a trunkful of books stored under the bed and that I would be allowed to read them 'when you are a big girl'. She had no idea that I could read both English and Welsh fluently. But Sara and Mari knew.

The Bible that was used during David's funeral remained on the dressing table. I opened it, and written on the front page in copper-plate writing were the following words:

Awarded to Myfanwy Lloyd-Williams
by members of St Michael's Church
on her departure to Saint Edmunds College,
September 1906

'Mamo, is this your Bible?'
'Yes, why?'
'Are you Myfanwy Lloyd-Williams?'
Silence – an uncomfortable silence.
'Answer me, Mamo.'
'That Myfanwy is no more, she was buried in her own guilt, a long, long time ago.'
'What do you mean? Is she dead?'
'Yes, in a way. You are too young to under-

stand Jini *fach*, but you will one day when you are grown up.'

Her lips tightened, and I knew I would be told no more. I would have gathered a great deal of knowledge by the time I 'grew up', but they would be surprised if they knew how much information I had already accumulated by putting two and two together.

One day when I came home from school, I saw the Rector's pony tied to the gate, and he was inside talking to Mamo. I listened outside the door. 'The two girls will be company for each other. Caroline is a very lonely child.'

I sensed that they were plotting some sort of scheme, so I entered the house.

Mamo smiled at me, a nervous, guilty smile, and said, 'The Rector has come to offer us a proposal, Jini. He is giving you the chance to have lessons at the Rectory along with his daughter Caroline, under a private tutor. You are a very lucky girl Jini.'

'What about school?'

'You won't have to attend school – these lessons at the Rectory are far, far superior to the lessons at school.'

Then the Rector added in his high and mighty voice, 'You will have the added benefit of being taught through the medium of English. It will do you good.'

'We are taught in English at the school,' said I.

'But this will be different,' said Mamo uneasily.

The parson snorted impatiently and said, 'You won't hear a word of Welsh spoken all day long, and you will be taught to speak, read and write English perfectly. It will do you a lot of good.'

I didn't want to be taught English perfectly, and no one could teach English better than Miss Evans. I sat in the corner and pouted. It was obvious that everything had been arranged and Mamo, unfortunately, thought that it was all for my good.

The Rector got up, and as he departed said in his I-know-best voice, 'Goodbye. I shall see you at the Rectory Monday morning at nine o'clock sharp. Don't be late Jane. Come to the back door.'

And away he went – he and his pony.

I ran down to Glan-dŵr to relate to them my tale of woe, fully expecting sympathy, and sugar on my bread-and-butter. But no – they too thought that I was 'a very lucky little girl'.

So to the Rectory I went early the following Monday morning. I met my friends on their way to school, and I had to explain to them about the 'do-you-good' school. They laughed, and called me Lady Jini. They left me standing, with tears running down my cheeks, whilst they ran helter-skelter, playing 'calico-she', as they hopped along.

I had never been to the Rectory before that day. I knocked nervously at the back door, and I could hear the savage bark of a dog from somewhere inside. A young girl wearing a sack apron, and her hair tied in a kerchief opened the door. I was led to a tiny room, with only one small window at the end – and there stood a tall scraggy woman, her hair plaited tightly in a bun, looking stern and sour. She reminded me of Miss!

'Come in Jane. Miss Caroline has not yet arrived. I am Miss Pickford.'

I noticed that I was just plain Jane, but that Caroline had the title Miss stuck on to her name.

Thus began my 'do-you-good' education, with the three of us sitting around a small round table on hard three-legged stools.

'Prayers to begin with.'

There never was any such nonsense at Bryn School; it was always tables or mental arithmetic to start off, followed by reading. I watched Caroline, and tried to do as she did. Hands together, eyes closed, and we chanted together a short prayer.

O Lord, Our Heavenly Father,
Teach me how to pray,
Make me sorry for my faults
For all I've done, amidst this day,
Give me grace to be thankful
For ever and ever, Amen.

Reading followed, not from a story book, but from the Bible. Miss Pickford first, then Caroline. She could not read a single word without Miss Pickford's help. I was next, and I read every word with ease. All Miss Pickford said was, 'Jane, you are showing off; I will not have that in my class.'

Then we had sums. Miss Pickford called the lesson 'arithmetic' – simple, childish sums, whilst Miss Evans had taught us to 'borrow the tens' and 'carry the tens'.

We copied sentences from the blackboard – I could hardly read Miss Pickford's writing; Miss Evans had taught us to press heavily, on the down stroke, and lightly on the up stroke. Then Miss Pickford read us a silly story about the Prince and a witch. She went on and on, for a long, long time in a harsh flat voice. I felt tired and hungry.

Mamo had prepared a packed lunch for me, but I was allowed to 'dine' with the family and Miss Pickford. Even at table Miss Pickford had to interfere. 'Take your elbows off the table, child, do as Miss Caroline does.'

We had prayers again, led by the Rector this time, and then dinner. I did enjoy the food – meat, potatoes, cabbage and gravy, followed by a milk pudding. That, indeed, was the best part of my 'do-you-good' education.

And so it went on, day after day after day. Passing my schoolfriends on my way every morning, and having to suffer being called a 'snob' and a 'swankie'.

But one morning I got really fed up – I turned around and accompanied them to school. Miss Evans was surprised to see me, but all she said was, 'Does your mother know Jini?', and all I said was 'not yet.'

I was afraid to go home, because Mamo truly thought that the lessons I received at the Rectory would be of everlasting benefit to me. But the parson had forestalled me, and according to him, 'I was a difficult child and inclined to show off.'

Obviously he was repeating what the Pickford had told him.

Poor Mamo, she was so quiet; I could see the sadness in her eyes. I had disappointed her, and I was very sorry, but on the other hand glad that I would never again be taught by that awful woman. Thus ended my 'do-you-good' education.

Back again at my old school, eating dry sandwiches and drinking cold milk, but having Miss Evans as my teacher made up for the posh dinners and the sweet puddings.

I was in my element in Standard III with Miss Evans, and I felt sorry for Caroline having to put up with Miss Pickford's dry-as-dust lessons. Caroline had no idea of the fun we had playing with friends. She had never heard of our games – games of 'Bugaboo in the well', 'Roll of tobacco' and 'Tail catch tail'.

She had never heard our witches' rhyme, which we sang in order to choose a leader:

> Inc a binc a be la-ga,
> Aitch, yo, ela ma-la
> Inc a binc a be la-ga,
> Out goes she.

I told Mamo that, but all she said was, 'You needn't worry about Caroline. Miss Pickford is only paid to teach her deportment – she will attend a residential school when she will be ten, and then she will have plenty of friends.'

I had no idea what 'deportment' meant; but if that was what they called Miss Pickford's teaching, then God help Caroline, poor thing.

'You won't send me away to school, will you Mamo?'

'No Jini – unfortunately I cannot afford to do so.'

'Thanks be to God,' I muttered quietly, and I was certain Dyta would have agreed with me.

We seldom saw him after David's death. Mamo said that he worked on a farm in Pembrokeshire and lived with his mother. Occasionally he would arrive home very late on a Saturday night, and leave again Sunday morning. He slept in the attic and Mamo saw to it that the bedroom door was well and truly bolted.

I attended school regularly, and enjoyed every minute of every day. But one afternoon I had a terrible shock – a terrible shock indeed. The Master came to inspect our writing books, and without even saying one word to Miss Evans, proclaimed in his rough, loud voice, 'Jini John, you are to move up to Standard IV. Come to my class on Monday morning.'

And, after that day, my life was never again the same.

16

The Master was a cruel old man – we were all terrified of him. He sported a huge gold ring on the little finger of his right hand; he would thump the children viciously, and sometimes the ring would catch and scrape the skin off our hands and arms, spattering blood everywhere.

I tried every excuse to stay at home that Monday morning. I had a valid excuse too – stomach-ache – but Mamo was deaf to my plea.

I arrived at school sick and unhappy, and I tried another dodge. I walked head-high straight into Miss Evans's class, and sat down in my usual place, hoping that he might have forgotten everything about me. But no such luck; as soon as I sat down there was a roar, like a bull's roar, 'Jini John, did I not tell you to come to my class today?'

The stomach-ache became worse and I had to ask to go to the 'go-out'. There I stayed for a long time, crying myself sick.

When I returned he seemed quieter and kinder, and I was given a new copy book, and a brand new pen and nib, but I had to write everything on a slate first, and then copy it out in my best handwriting in my book. If I did not hold the pen correctly in my right hand with my thumb and two fingers held straight, down would come the ruler, bang, on my hand. But I must be honest, and confess that life was not as bad as I had feared. By mid-morning playtime my stomach-ache had disappeared.

Once a month the 'nit-nurse' would visit the school to inspect our hair. I hated her – she looked too much like Miss, and the Pickford, for my liking – a tall, gaunt woman wearing thick spectacles, and a navy-blue cap folded tightly on her head with the ends hanging down her back. She would unplait my hair in a rough way, examine it carefully with a tooth comb, and allow me to go, without uttering one word.

Mamo looked after my hair – she washed it regularly; I was proud of my hair.

But everybody did not have such tender care. I remember little Sali Pennar being sent home in tears, and the nurse shouting at her as she left, 'I shall call at your home this evening around six. Tell your mother to sharpen the scissors.'

We all knew what that meant. Sali had the most beautiful mop of hair – golden curls, the colour of the broom. She was the prettiest girl in school.

The following day she arrived back, wearing a tight woollen cap to hide her baldness. The 'nit-nurse' had shaved her curls away. She was not pretty little Sali any more, but a dull stupid child who stood in the corner, and who refused to talk or play with us. Some of the daft boys would poke fun at her and call her 'sheep's head'. If the Master asked her a question – any sort of simple question – she would burst into tears. She had to stand in the corner for hours on end, and instead of asking to go to the 'go-out' she would pee on the floor. The 'nit-nurse' and the Master between them completely ruined her life. She was never the same again, not even after her hair had re-grown. She remained shy and timid, and was placed in the *'twps'* class. The Master ignored them completely – they had to fend for themselves, and see to their own education. On the other hand he worked hard with those children who were considered bright, 'who had plenty in their heads', and emphasised the importance of passing the 'Scholarship', and entrance to the County School 'in order to bring merit to our school and have a good job in life, away from this back-of-beyond'.

At the back of the class sat three or four 'big girls' – they were fourteen-year-olds, and ready to leave. He would spend a great deal of his time sitting with these girls pretending to teach them, but really it was just an excuse to play with them – pushing his hands up under their clothes and tickling their breasts, and if anyone dared to turn back to have a peep, they received a mighty box on the ear. It was safer to keep your distance from the Master, but of course that was impossible in a cramped classroom. We were all frightened of him – apart from the girls on the back benches.

We had two play yards and two shelters to protect us from the bad weather – one for the boys and one for the girls, with a high stone wall separating them. Sometimes the big boys would climb the intervening wall and tease the girls, but if the Master happened to catch them – look out: down would come the cane from the top of the cupboard. He only used the cane on special occasions; thumping and walloping were usually the order of the day.

The 'go-outs' were at the furthest end of the yard – three compartments, one for the teachers, and two for us girls. The boys' 'go-outs' were on the other side of the wall. There was no running water. The solids were contained in buckets, but we were ordered to pee in the gutter which ran the length of the 'go-outs'. Apparently, according to the Master, that was better for our health, and also saved the cleaner's time. So for the sake of our health and the cleaning woman's time, we had to 'pass water' in the gutter, which was bone dry for most of the year – it had running water only when it rained.

Yet in spite of all the drawbacks – the distance to school, the dry sandwiches, the Master's temper, the stench in the 'go-outs', the fun and games in the playground – the teaching we received at the Board School was far superior to the lessons I had at the 'do-you-good' school.

About once a year the Inspector would pay the school a visit. He was a tall, elegant man with white hair and a kindly smile. The Master would collect our copy books and sum books for inspection. Only the 'top class' were allowed to write in copy books, the *'twps'* wrote on slates. He would then call upon us to read in English, and translate a few sentences into Welsh – we were also tested in 'mental sums' and 'general knowledge'. The Inspector spoke to us in Welsh, and the Master followed suit, but only for that one day, unfortunately.

Apart from the Inspector, no visitors called at our school. Mamo was surprised to hear that, because when she was a little girl at her school, the Rector would call every week, and they had prayers and hymn singing every morning – we had mental sums and reading.

But one morning, instead of our daily dose of mental sums and tables, the Master invited

Miss Evans's class and the 'babies' class to join the 'top class'. He delivered a long-winded speech about Lloyd George, and to our surprise he spoke quite a lot of Welsh, because 'it is very important that everybody understands so that you can carry the message home.'

It was a boring talk – 'but for Lloyd George the Germans would have invaded Great Britain and would have murdered every man, woman and child, yes, even tiny babies. We must all respect and thank such a great man. And because he is a Welshman we, above all, should be proud of him.'

He carried on and on about Lloyd George and his wonderful qualities before, at last, coming to the point. Lloyd George and his wife would be visiting our village that very day at two o'clock. He was coming because there was to be an election in Cardiganshire in a week's time, and Lloyd George's best friend would be standing as a Liberal candidate in that election. There was another Liberal candidate opposing him but he was a dead loss, of no consequence whatsoever. We would be allowed out of school to meet the Lloyd Georges and the candidate, and we were to yell together in one big shout 'Lloyd George for ever'.

All morning we practised the 'shout' until we were all hoarse. Wili Weirglodd knew a verse about the election, and we learnt that too:

Lloyd George for ever!
He fought the war to make us free.
We'll hang Llywelyn Williams
On a sour apple tree.

Llywelyn Williams was the other contestant, and the Master thought it was a good verse.

The Lloyd George party did not arrive until four o'clock, and we had lost our voices by that time. Mr Lloyd George looked like any other man, but Mrs Lloyd George was a beautiful lady. She had a long fur scarf around her neck, which almost touched her toes.

A crowd had waited patiently to see them – a few waved their Union Jack flags. Lloyd George spoke for a few minutes – someone had timed him – Ernest Evans the candidate did not open his mouth. A shy little girl presented Mrs Lloyd George with a posy of flowers. She accepted the flowers graciously and asked her, 'What is your name, my dear?'

'Mair Eluned.'

She lifted the child in her arms and hugged her. As she handed her back to her mother, she said tearfully, 'Look after her well – I lost my Mair Eluned.'

There were tears all around, because it was a well-known fact that Mr and Mrs Lloyd George had lost a daughter called Mair Eluned.

One of the party threw some sweets into the

air, which developed into a game of 'catch-as-catch-can'.

They departed in a hurry, and we were too busy trying to grab the sweets to shout 'Lloyd George for ever' as they went.

A few days later, Llywelyn Williams (the other Liberal candidate) arrived in the village – but we were not allowed to meet him.

The election was fun. It was the talk of the parish – people argued and quarrelled over the election. We played 'election' at school, and Ernest Evans won every time. Sara and Mari were not on speaking terms; Mamo supported Ernest Evans, but she didn't have a vote. Dyta came all the way from Pembrokeshire on his wonky bike to vote for Llywelyn Williams, because 'he is a bloody great man, and the workingman's friend.'

Ernest Evans won, and Dyta was very disappointed; he called the Cardis 'a lot of bloody nincompoops'. He blamed Lloyd George for his lameness, and back he went to Pembrokeshire 'where lived sensible people innit, who knew what was what.'

17

The Master was taken ill very suddenly, very ill indeed – he was admitted to hospital and Miss Evans had to teach the top class as well as her own. Miss remained aloof in her own classroom, and gave her no help at all. Miss Evans carried on as well as she could; there was no sign of the Master returning.

But one day a pleasant young man appeared from nowhere and took over the top class. He came from North Wales apparently; he spoke with a funny sort of accent, exactly as if he had a hot potato in his mouth. He was so different from the Master in every way – he spoke to us in Welsh, laughed with us, and told funny jokes. We called him 'Sir', so as not to confuse him with the Master.

The first morning after his arrival, he told us to take out our copy books, and when only about half of us took out books – the others had slates – he wanted to know why.

'Because they are *twps*, Sir – they're blockheads.'

He became very quiet, and there was a sad look on his face. Eventually he said, 'Don't, I beg of you, call any child a *twp* in my hearing again. I am ashamed of you.'

'The Master calls them *twps*, Sir,' we shouted.

'I am the master now, and I don't want anyone, not anyone, calling a child by that disgusting name again. Understand?'

Yes, we all understood; and he gave us a lecture about the fact that every child was different, and how some excelled in one subject, and others in another subject. Each and every child is endowed with a special talent, and no child is *twp*. In spite of his funny accent, we all understood him perfectly.

So each child was given a copy book and a pen, and during the reading lesson no one was passed by. He spent more time with the backward children than he did with the bright ones.

He brought a football to school and taught the boys how to play properly and keep to the rules. No cheating or squabbling. It was impossible to play any decent game in the girls' yard, so he used to take us occasionally to the boys' playground, and taught us to play rounders according to the rules.

He never punched us, neither did he slap us with the ruler. He frowned when he was displeased, and one day when Wili Weirglodd poked fun at one of the small boys and called him 'a bloody stupid idiot', he took him quietly to the porch, and gave him a good talking. When they came out Wili was in tears, and never again did he call any child by that name, not within Sir's hearing, at any rate.

We had prayers first thing every morning – we sang Welsh songs; he taught us to recite, and how to compose poetry. He told us stories about the great heroes of Wales; we read Welsh books – books that he found at the bottom of a cupboard, books smelling of mould and mildew.

Life was good during those days; it was sheer joy to attend school. I was never so happy, and Mamo seemed happier too. Auntie Mary came to visit every Tuesday, and Marged and her basket arrived every Friday. Dyta would arrive very late on Saturday, shuffle his way noisily up the ladder, stay in bed until dinner time on Sunday, and depart again for Pembrokeshire.

Mamo and I continued to sleep together in the big bed, and bolted the bedroom door every night. Dyta remained the same, no one could change Dyta. Whenever he came home he would curse, rant and rave and call Mamo a 'bloody eunuch', whatever that was supposed to mean. It puzzled me how Mamo managed to live without any means of support, because Dyta never gave her a penny piece. I overhead her asking him, 'How much do you earn now, Ifan?'

'Why do you ask?'

'I find it difficult to make ends meet, and Jini needs new clothes.'

'How the hell do you think I've got money to throw away on bloody clothes? Me? A man who suffers from war wounds – an ex-serviceman. Good God – the cheek of it!'

'The child is growing fast, Ifan – she badly needs a new winter coat.'

'You'll have to ask some other devil, someone who has more money than me.'

'You are hard, Ifan.'

'Me, hard? Who's put the bloody bolt on the door? And what's more, I live with my old mother, and I have to help her to pay the rent. You are lucky enough to have your house rent free, Miss Myfanwy.'

And away he would go, leaving Mamo depressed and straining to hold back the tears.

'Don't worry, Mamo *fach*, winter is another month away, and maybe Auntie Mary will buy me a new coat for Christmas.'

'No, no, that's wrong. We have depended far too heavily over the years on Auntie Mary and Marged. It is high time your father shouldered some of the responsibility.'

Mamo was quite the lady; so was Auntie Mary. They spoke nicely and never used bad language. What on earth possessed her to marry such a foul-mouthed creature as Dyta? Perhaps one day, when I was a 'big girl' I would get to the bottom of the mystery.

But I was happy in spite of not having a new

coat, and I prayed every night to God asking him to keep Dyta away for good, and to let Sir stay for evermore as our headmaster.

Now and again, on fine Saturdays, Mamo and I would walk over the hill, keeping to the postman's path, and arrive early at Pen-gwern, Auntie Mary's home. It was a wonderful place – they had everything there – all sorts of animals, big and small, dangerous and tame. They had cats, dogs, goats and donkeys, but my favourite was Flower, the white pony that I rode across the fields, my hair flying in the wind, and my heart beating faster and faster. Life was good, and I fancied myself as 'a lady' – I thought only 'ladies' rode horses.

But for Auntie Mary's friendship and kindness, life would have been far duller for Mamo. She still fretted after little David, and sometimes she would toss and turn in bed and weep silently.

'Mamo, perhaps it would be better for both of us if I went to sleep in the attic.'

'You will not go back to the attic, not as long as your father has the key to the front door.'

So we slept in the big bed, taking care to bolt the bedroom door every night.

It was drawing towards Christmas, and I was still in my old coat, but I didn't care, I had far more interesting things to think about.

Sir decided to hold a Christmas concert, and

every child was to take part. He called it a 'Miscellaneous Concert'. Miss called it a 'Penny Reading', and refused to allow her 'babies' to perform. It was said that she had told Sir that she had 'better work to do than to teach little children to make fools of themselves'.

Fun and excitement all day and every day; Miss Evans and the big girls working flat out, sewing and cutting-out costumes for the fairies and the gypsies, and the actors in the drama. Sir wrote the drama. It was all about the birth of Jesus, and I was chosen to take the part of Mary. I was dressed in Miss Evans's blue nightgown which trailed on the floor, and a blue-and-white striped cloth tied on my head. The baby Jesus was a soft cushion wrapped in a shawl. Wili Weirglodd was Joseph, because 'he had a strong voice, and thought a lot of himself.'

When the big night arrived the schoolroom was full to overflowing with an audience packed as tightly as sardines. Everyone was wound up – people were standing at the back, clapping, whistling and shouting 'encore'. The drama was the final item, and I was very nervous. I did not have a speaking part, but I had to nurse the baby and sing two carols. The first was:

Away in a manger, no crib for a bed
The little Lord Jesus laid down his sweet head.
The stars in the bright sky looked down where
    he lay,
The little Lord Jesus asleep on the hay.

The other was a Welsh carol:

> *Suai'r gwynt, suai'r gwynt*
> *Wrth fyned heibio'r drws,*
> *A Mair ar ei gwely gwair,*
> *Wyliai ei baban tlws.*
> *Syllai yn ddwys yn ei wyneb llon,*
> *Gwasgai Waredwr y byd at ei bron,*
> *Canai ddiddanol gân,*
> *Cwsg, cwsg, f'anwylyd bach,*
> *Cwsg nes daw'r bore iach.*

As I caressed the cushion in my arms, I forgot
that it was a cushion – a strange feeling possessed
me – the feeling that I was nursing a live baby,
and that I was holding little David in my arms.
I almost failed to utter the words, *'Cwsg, cwsg,
f'anwylyd bach'* (Sleep, sleep, my little one). My
voice cracked, and the tears started to roll. I
saw Sir smiling at me, and I knew I had to carry
on. I took a deep breath, and succeeded to
finish the song. Sir came to me and said, 'Jini,
you sang like an angel.'

There was complete silence for a few seconds,

and then the whole audience shouted 'Encore Jini, encore Jini.' But to my relief, Sir raised his arm, and we all sang *'Hen Wlad Fy Nhadau'*.

Sara and Mari were there to see me home. Mamo refused to come; she said that she had a cold. I was so anxious to tell her everything about the concert, but to my disappointment Dyta had arrived, and it was obvious that they had been quarrelling. Neither asked me how I had got on, and all Mamo said was, 'Jini, go to bed, it's late.'

But Dyta had to have the last word, and as I opened the bedroom door he shouted mockingly, 'And don't forget to bolt the bloody door.'

18

It was Christmas, and Mamo and I were the only ones to tuck into the turkey that Marged had brought in her basket. She brought more than the turkey – there were fruit, jam, cakes, nuts and vegetables also in the basket – enough food to last for weeks.

Dyta stayed with his mother 'the old woman, poor dab, would have been lonely on her own'. But really and truly, Mamo and I were inwardly pleased that he had stayed away. Towards evening, Auntie Mary arrived with more presents. She brought me a new winter overcoat with a fur collar just like the coat that Mrs Lloyd George had worn for the 'Lloyd George for ever' election. I felt like a real lady, walking around, swinging my hips, with my head held high. Never before had I received such a swanky, grown-up present. But Mamo was not at all pleased. All she said was, and that in a flat ungrateful voice, 'It is not your duty to clothe Jini, Mary.'

'No, of course not, but it is my duty to present my best friend with a gift for Christmas.'

Mamo was silent for a short while, and then said, trying hard to hold back the tears, 'I don't know what I would have done without you, Mary.'

'Tut, tut, don't talk nonsense. It won't be like this for ever, Myfi.'

'No Mary, I must learn to accept my fate. I made my own bed, and now I must lie on it. It was all my doing.'

Grown-up talk again, but I was beginning to get the gist of it, and trying my best to put two and two together – but they didn't always add up to four!

Auntie Mary brought Mamo a present too – a novel called 'The Woman Thou Gavest Me' by Hall Caine. It was left lying on the table, and I started to read it. It was a book for grown-ups, but I became engrossed in it. It was far more interesting than Mamo and Auntie Mary's chatter.

I was unwilling to attend school the following week, because Mari had heard in the village that the Master had recovered and that he would be back in school the following Monday. But to our joy what should we see propped against the school wall that morning but Sir's bike. It is amazing how the presence of one person can make a difference to a child's well-being.

Every child in school thought the world of him. Miss Evans got on well with him too, but I don't know about Miss. She kept to her room, and Sir never entered her quarters. It was wiser to keep your distance where Miss was concerned!

The Master never listened to children's complaints, not even when two boys fought like young cocks, with their blood spattered around; but Sir listened to every tale of woe, and had a special way of dealing with the bully.

The first lesson on the first day of the first term involved telling Sir how we had spent Christmas. The chapel children described how they had sung and recited at the children's meeting, and the church children how they had sung carols at the *Plygain*. But I had nothing to say, because I attended neither church nor chapel.

'Jini, I'm sure you did something. Did Santa Claus call at your house?'

I just could not tell him that he hadn't – although I was expecting him, and although I knew it was all a big fraud. When Auntie Mary asked me the same question, Mamo replied curtly, 'Jini is a big girl now, she does not believe in such childish nonsense.' I was 'a big girl' when it suited Mamo.

I could not tell Sir all that, but I did tell him that I'd had a new coat just like Mrs Lloyd George's coat, and that I had read an English novel called 'The Woman Thou Gavest Me' from beginning to end.

He looked at me in surprise and said, 'Jini, you are indeed a wonder child. Keep at it, my girl, and you will soon be writing a novel yourself.'

Sir was a lovely man, and always praised us.

A fortnight later, what we all had feared happened. The bike was not leaning against the wall, and inside, the Master sat on his three legged stool, looking like the devil himself. His hair was greasy as always, but greyer and thinner, and his pot belly which used to hang over the top of his trousers had completely vanished. But he was the Master, there was no doubt about that, and without a word of explanation he began with the usual rigmarole – tables and spellings – huge words – words that we had no idea of their meanings like 'pentahedron', 'thermodynamics' and 'valetudinarian'

v-a-l-e = vale
v-a-l-e-t-u = valetu
v-a-l-e-t-u-d-i-n = valetudin
v-a-l-e-t-u-d-i-n-a-r-i-a-n = valetudinarian.

Then reading aloud – the same old tattered books, and as usual he passed by the slow learners. So very bravely, I piped up, thinking I should enlighten him on how things were at present. 'The *twps* can read now, Master,' I said.

Full stop – everything and everyone stopped. He looked daggers at me, glared at me for two or three minutes – minutes that seemed like hours, and said, 'Jini John, when I need your advice I shall ask for it. In the meantime, go and stand in the corner, and stay there until you can behave yourself, you forward hussy.'

And there I stood in the corner, biting my nails until 'small playtime' arrived.

The Master was a cruel old man, and his sickness had not changed him one little bit.

Life at school was back to normal once more, and but for the experience we'd had under the headship of Sir, I would have continued to believe that education was some kind of sickness one had to suffer, like the measles or the chickenpox.

Life at home was not very bright either. Mamo seemed low and depressed, and since Christmas she suffered from one cold after another. She would retire early every night and I would prepare a light supper for both of us – bread-and-butter and cheese or a boiled egg. Mamo had no appetite whatsoever, she picked at her food, and ate no more than a tom-tit.

At last I was allowed to rummage in the chest under the bed, and found the most wonderful books like *David Copperfield*, *Jane Eyre* and *The Mill on the Floss*. Every night I read and I read and Mamo had to shout angrily to get me to bed. Sometimes I would read the Bible – the English Bible – but somehow it did not appeal to me half as much as the big Bible at Glan-dŵr.

Every Saturday I would go to Glan-dŵr to read

the *Tivy-side* and tried to memorise as much as I could, so as to relate all the news to Mamo.

I could not bear Saturday nights and Sunday mornings. That was when Dyta came home to disturb the peace. They quarrelled all the time. Mamo was often in tears, especially if she had begged him for money. He would then curse and rave and call her a 'bloody snob'.

'The finest piece of work I ever did in my life was to bring you down a peg or two to the level of the working class. Good God, woman, I did you a great kindness, and you should bloody well thank me for it, instead of grovelling.'

He expected a cooked supper ready for him on a Saturday night – then away to some unknown place. Sometimes he would stay away all night long, other times he would return during the early hours, and he could never resist the temptation to give our bedroom door a mighty kick as he passed by. He would stay in bed until dinner time, then off to Pembrokeshire. And peace would reign once more.

At school we had to work very hard – common fractions, common interest, parsing, composition – on and on without end. I was lucky in a way to be included in the top class, otherwise I would have had to sit with the *twps* – writing on a slate, then rubbing it out, which meant spitting on the slate, drying it with one's sleeve, before writing the same thing over and over again.

We all fretted after Sir, especially the girls. As soon as he had gone, the big boys started on their bullying and nasty habits again. The smaller girls were really terrified – the boys would run after us showing their 'pieces', catching us, and pushing us against the stone wall. Wili Weirglodd was the leader; he swore just like Dyta, but the Master never punished him. May Penbryn said that he would not dare punish Wili, because his father was a County Councillor.

One day, the Master announced in class. 'Jini John and Johnnie Williams will have to stay behind every playtime, and for an hour after school, every day, because I have decided to enter them both for the Scholarship exam, and for that they must have extra lessons.'

Attending school was a misery at the best of times; from now on it would be ten times worse. In my own mind I could think of no better way of describing it than to use Dyta's down-to-earth language 'fuck the bloody Scholarship'.

I would not have dared, no not even to whisper that kind of language to anyone but myself. No, nor to any other living person. I would have been too ashamed.

19

Time dragged on – from day to day, from month to month, until Christmas arrived once again and even that day was no different from any other day. No grand school concert, no Santa Claus and no presents. But Marged brought her basket laden with food as usual.

I had outgrown 'Mrs Lloyd George's coat', but Mamo stripped it of the fur, found an old coat that used to belong to her, shortened it, moved the buttons, made tucks where necessary and stitched back the fur. I felt quite the lady once again; it was the fur that made it special.

Since the Master had proclaimed that I was to sit the Scholarship, life had become a burden – staying in school during 'small playtime' and part of the dinner hour, writing compositions endlessly, re-writing them again and again until they were absolutely perfect – and these on the most uninteresting subjects like the 'League of Nations'. I can still remember the first sentence – 'The League of Nations was formed with the purpose of diminishing wars, and if possible to banish them altogether'.

The Master gave out a deafening cry, 'Not *with* the purpose, you blockhead, but *for* the purpose. Watch your prepositions.'

I remember writing other compositions on equally dull subjects, for example, 'The Education of Adults' and 'The aim of the Sunday School'. I had never attended Sunday School in my life, so how could I write about its aim? But I need not have worried: when he saw my feeble attempt he wrote the composition himself, and I had to learn it off by heart.

His standard of education was very high. He was strong and healthy once again, his belly was the same size as of old, and his moustache hung down limply over his upper lip. He continued to tickle the big girls' knees, and one day he gave me the same treatment. I shrieked. Everyone stared, and he whispered under his breath, 'You must learn to control yourself, you little devil. Never do that again.'

It was he who needed to control himself, not me.

One day I asked Mamo if I could move back to sleep in the loft.

'No,' – a very definite 'no'.

Why Mamo?'

'What if your father decided to return suddenly?'

'He never comes home during the week, Mamo.'

'You can't depend on your father, and I can never trust him again, not as long as I live. And don't you trust him either. Do you promise?'

'Yes, Mamo,' and I really meant it.

'On your honour?'

'Yes, Mamo, on my honour.'

But I continued to worry, and Mamo continued to cough.

I had a bright idea. I would ask Mari Rees what the black medicine was.

'Mari, what's in that stuff that you give Mamo to drink?'

'That is the best medicine anyone can take to cure coughs and colds. It has no name, it is just a cure for coughs.'

'Yes, I know. But what does it contain? What have you put in it?'

'Well, if you must know, the main ingredient is comfrey. That is the best possible cure for the cough, better than any doctor's medicine. Are you satisfied now?'

'Yes, Mari, thank you. I have every faith in your ability as a healer.'

At the first opportunity I proposed to look up 'comfrey' in Mari's big doctor book. That book gave the meaning and purpose of every growing plant. I knew that Friday was Mari's day for collecting plants, so off I went to Glan-dŵr the minute I came home from school.

Sara was at home on her own, and luckily the big red book was on the dresser by the big Bible. I knew that not even Sara was allowed to browse in that book. It was holier than the Bible itself in Mari's opinion. She was the authority on every sickness and pain. There was only one person in the whole parish who knew more than she did, and that was Doctor Powell, and even he, the doctor himself, was known to have asked for her advice when everything else had failed.

'Sara, may I have a peep at the doctor's book?'

'Mari does not like anyone to touch that book?'

'Why, Sara?'

'It is a very dangerous book for those who know nothing about plants and diseases. She usually keeps it under the bed, but she forgot to put it back today.'

'Just one tiny peep, Sara?'

'Alright, but don't tell Mari that I allowed you to touch it.'

'Not one word, Sara, I promise, criss-cross, and hope to die.'

I found it without trouble.

'Comfrey. Government and virtues. It belongs to Mercury, and according to Dioscorides, when boiled with strong ale and treacle it can ease the cough, and cure the consumption in its early stages.'

Consumption! My stomach somersaulted, my heart stopped. I knew full well what that meant; to suffer from the consumption meant certain death. Was that the reason for that dreadful cough? Mari must have thought so, or she would not have dosed her with comfrey. I decided to call the doctor, and that at once. It would be of no use whatsoever to talk to Dyta. His gammy leg and the bolt on the door were his only worries; he did not care about Mamo, not one little bit. If Auntie Mary didn't call before the end of the week, I would walk all the way to Pen-gwern along the postman's path. But fortunately she called the following Friday afternoon.

'Jini, you look so miserable. Smile child.'

'I am miserable Auntie Mary, and I cannot smile.'

'What's wrong my dear?'

'Mamo.'

'Does she continue to cough?'

'Yes, all night, and every night. She has caught the consumption.'

'What? Who told you that?'

'I read it in Mari's big doctor book.'

I could see that Auntie Mary was disturbed. 'But you can't be certain, just by reading Mari's doctor book.'

'But the medicine that Mari gives her is made out of comfrey, and that is the herb for curing the consumption. I read it myself.'

'Nonsense. What does she know. She is not a doctor.'

'No, that is why we must call the doctor at once. God only knows where we shall find money to pay him.'

Don't worry, Jini. Dr Powell will only be too glad to come. He thinks the world of your mother.'

That was a comfort. But Mamo continued to cough and spit without stop.

The following day was a Saturday, and to my joy Dr Powell and Auntie Mary arrived together in style in the governess trap, complete with a big black bag.

Mamo was in bed as usual and the doctor and Auntie Mary entered the bedroom. I followed.

'Jini,' said Auntie Mary, 'stay outside for the time being, you shall come in after the doctor has finished his examination.'

Examination? What was the meaning of that? She must be very ill to require an examination. I didn't like the sound of it.

And there they were for ages, whilst I was in the kitchen, waiting, waiting – hoping for the best, but fearing the worst.

But who should arrive earlier than usual but Dyta, sweating like a pig, and stinking of farm manure. 'Good lord, hell's bells. What's going on? What is that bloody carnival outside?'

'The doctor is here, and he is giving Mamo a thorough examination.'

'Examination! Bloody hell! It's me that should have an examination innit?'

'Mamo is very ill, Dyta. She is coughing day and night.'

'I know she coughs. *Diawl* – we all cough when we have a cold. Why the bloody fuss? Examination, indeed! Good lord.'

At that Dr Powell appeared, looked at Dyta and said solemnly, 'I want a word with you, Ifan. Come outside.'

And out they went. Auntie Mary came into the kitchen and had a far-away look in her eyes.

'Yes, Auntie Mary, what did the doctor say.'

Dead silence followed.

Then she spoke slowly and carefully as if measuring her words. 'Your mother is very ill, Jini. She is weak and worn out with all the coughing.'

'I know that, Auntie Mary. Has she caught the consumption?'

'The doctor didn't say that, but he said it could develop into consumption, if the coughing does not ease.'

'Auntie Mary, I want the truth. Does Mamo suffer from consumption? The truth, Auntie Mary.'

She did not reply, but embraced me tenderly, and I could see tears running down her cheeks. Then she said, 'Jini, I shall do all I can to help her, and to help you too. I shall look after you both. I promise you. Let God be my witness.'

I'd had my answer – there was no need to ask any more questions. Mamo suffered from that deadly disease, called consumption.

20

Without doubt, Mamo suffered from consumption, or 'the decline', as we all called it, and neither I, nor anyone else dared to mention the word aloud; we only felt it, down in the depths of our souls. I went to school daily, pretending that all was well – playing 'calico she' as usual; staying in school after hours preparing for the Scholarship, and sweating over my homework for hours at home.

On the face of it, everything was the same, but the worry kept gnawing inside, until it felt like a sickness, an incurable sickness like the decline.

'How's your mother, Jini *fach*?'

'She's getting better slowly.'

The lie slipped easily from the tongue. But the way people asked spoke volumes; you could hear the pity and the sympathy in the way they uttered 'Jini *fach*'. 'Decline' was like a swear word, a word to avoid.

Auntie Mary would call round three days a week, Marged as always on a Friday, and Dyta had taken into his head to arrive home on Friday night and stay until Sunday. Why, I don't know, because he was away again within minutes after arriving.

One weekend he arrived home on a stinking, noisy motor-bike.

'Ifan, where did you find the money to pay for that horrible machine?'

'Good God woman, is that how you thank me for making the effort to come home? I only paid seven pounds for it, and I pay that at the rate of half-a-crown a week, so shut your bloody gob.'

She didn't have the strength to argue. After Dr Powell had 'a word' with Dyta he seemed more subdued, his language was not quite so lurid as it used to be: that is apart from the word 'bloody'. That little word was part and parcel of his everyday language – 'the bloody weather', 'the bloody parson'. But on the whole his language was more sober, and his manner more seemly. He continued to sleep in the attic, but he now climbed quietly, and refrained from kicking the bedroom door as he passed.

Mamo insisted that we both shared the same bed, but one day Auntie Mary brought me a camp bed, and suggested that I should sleep in the kitchen. But no – Mamo was adamant. And I knew why without asking.

I was very unhappy at school; the Master was a real slave-driver. Johnnie and I were kept at it for hours every day, long after the other children had gone home.

'You two, if you stick at it, will bring credit to the school, to your headmaster, and to yourselves. I shall retire soon, and you will probably be my last Scholarship candidates.'

No. He didn't care about us, neither did he care about the school – he cared only about his image and position in the chapel and in the community. After all, he was a deacon in the chapel, but at heart he was a selfish, pompous and conceited old man.

He never appeared outside in the playground and knew nothing of the bullying and cruelty the big boys inflicted on the younger ones. Wili Weirglodd was the head bandit, he used to frighten the girls too – run after us and catch us, press us against the wall and show us his billy. He used to run after the little boys with his rusty knife and pretend to chop off their billies. 'I'll castrate you'.

It was useless complaining about him, because Wili's father was still a County Councillor and friendly with the Master. Wili didn't have to sit the Scholarship, because his father was a wealthy man, and at fourteen he would attend Llanymddyfri College, where all the toffs went, and not the County School where all the riff-raff were educated.

But one day, Wili was beaten good and proper, not by the Master, but by the most harmless, most insignificant boy in the whole school. Guto Pen-lan considered himself to be a poet of some standing. When Sir was the Head he taught us about rhyme and metre, and Guto became a bard overnight. One day he proudly brought to school a poem written by himself, and asked us to learn it off by heart, and to repeat it loudly whenever Wili was within earshot.

> Wili has a tiny billy
> Smaller much than Bili's billy,
> Bili's billy is big and fat
> Wili's billy is thin and squat.

(Bili was the he-goat that grazed in a field nearby).

It was a silly nonsensical rhyme but it did the trick. Instead of infuriating Wili, as we all feared it would, he became as flat as a pancake, and whenever Wili would start on his antics, we would shout Guto's poem until the whole place echoed, and Wili would fade quietly out of sight. It was amazing how a small, innocent boy was able to sweep the floor with the biggest bully in school. It was just as I had read in one of Mamo's books, 'the pen is mightier than the sword'. Bravo Guto!

One day I had a dreadful experience – an experience which shattered me, body and soul; an experience that I shall never forget as long as

I live. Johnnie was absent and I thought that there would be no 'stay behind' that day, for the extra lesson to prepare us for the sacred Scholarship. When I was in the porch, on the point of leaving, the Master called me back and asked me to stand by the wall. There I stood like a statue against the wall for fifteen minutes or more, until everyone had cleared. There wasn't a soul around. He approached me and placed his arm around my shoulder, played with my plaits, and started to unpick them. My heart stopped. I began to sweat. He pressed himself against me and said in Welsh, 'Jini you are a pretty girl. Give me a kiss, my sweet one.'

I was paralysed; I could not utter a word. His lips were pressed against my lips – his breath reeked of stale tobacco. I felt sick. Then he pressed me still harder against the wall, tore the buttons off my jersey and the straps off my bodice, and kissed my body like a madman. His greasy moustache nearly smothered me. I nearly fainted, I felt like retching and I could hardly breathe.

But worse was to come. He tore the elastic off my bloomers and they fell on the floor. I couldn't move; I was crying hysterically by this time. He then started to undress – he unbuttoned his trousers using one hand, the other hand he had across my mouth to stop me from screaming. Panic stricken, I struggled. I bit his hand and found my voice. I shouted, 'Someone's knocking on the door.'

I had lied of course, but mercifully he believed me. He stopped to listen. I saw my chance. I ran out through the other door, leaving my bloomers on the floor.

I was free. I ran panting, without stopping for breath, like a bat out of hell. I avoided the village, paddled through the stream; scrambled over hedges, ran across the fields and arrived home breathless like a frightened rabbit escaping from the jaws of the greyhound. Who should be outside Llety'r Wennol when I arrived but Auntie Mary. She gasped when she saw me. I must have been a sorry sight, sweating profusely, tears running down my cheeks, my hair dishevelled, and feeling so ashamed.

'Jini, what's happened? Are you ill? Did you fall? Who has abused you? Who Jini? Tell me. You must tell me.'

I was dumb and numb from fright. I didn't want to tell. I felt the shame of it deeply.

She embraced me tenderly. That helped to ease the pain inside me slightly – a pain that kept on gnawing and gripping. My jersey was still unbuttoned, the straps of my bodice torn and my bloomers missing.

'You must tell me, Jini my dear. You *must*.'

'The Master, Auntie Mary.'

'The Headmaster?'

'Yes.'

'The dirty devil.'

'You don't often swear, Auntie Mary.'

'I didn't swear, Jini. I only called the beast by his rightful name.'

'Don't tell Mamo – please Auntie Mary.'

'No, I shan't tell your mother, but someone should be told. What about your father?'

'No, no, not Dyta. Please Auntie Mary, don't tell anybody – not a soul. I shall deal with it on my own.'

'Jini *fach*, how can you do that – he is a dangerous man.'

'I shall go on strike, like the colliers. I shall refuse to sit the Scholarship.'

'You will upset your mother by doing that – she is quite determined that you will go to the County School.'

'No, I can't upset Mamo.'

'Oh, Jini, you are a brave little girl. Where's your coat and your school bag.'

'They are all in school in the girls' porch. When I had the chance, I ran leaving everything behind. I left my bloomers too – there was no time to pick it up from the floor.'

Auntie Mary was in tears, and so was I. Then we looked at each other, and suddenly we both laughed. We imagined the Master answering the door, how he had been fooled, and the bloomers on the floor as evidence to

162

remind him of his wicked ways. That laugh broke the ice – it was not a happy laugh, it was more of a spiteful laugh, the result of a sort of pride in myself that I'd got the better of him.

'It will be easy to hide what has happened from your mother. She is in bed and has been all day. I'll have a word with Miss Evans and ask her to collect your coat and bag.

'Don't tell her the whole story, Auntie Mary.'

'All right, if you say so. But someone should be told.'

'No, Auntie Mary, please no. It's our secret.'

She did not reply, but thanks be to Auntie Mary, thanks for her understanding and love. But my mind was made up. I was determined to stay at home the following day, and the day after, and the day following that too.

Auntie Mary was on the point of leaving and suddenly I felt lonely and dispirited.

'Auntie Mary, must you go? Stay awhile to talk to me.'

We were both leaning on the gate leading to the road, out of Mamo's hearing and out of the world's sight.

'Yes dear, what do you want to talk about?'

'How long has Mamo to live?'

Silence. But I could almost hear her thinking, and making up her mind about what to tell me.

'She is suffering from the decline, isn't she, Auntie Mary?'

'Maybe, but that does not mean that she will die.'

'Auntie Mary, be honest. No one can cure the decline – it is beyond all cure.'

'Some do, Jini – if it's caught in time.'

'But Mamo is growing weaker by the day, and the cough is growing worse and worse.'

She didn't reply. She knew as well as I did that she could not possibly last much longer.

'Auntie Mary, what will become of me after Mamo dies?'

'Listen Jini. Whatever happens in the future, I shall be here to look after you.'

'But I can't carry on to live at Llety'r Wennol.'

'But your father will be here to take care of you.'

'Auntie Mary, I want you to understand this, and I am really serious, I mean what I say. After Mamo dies I will have to look for a place on my own, because I can never, never live alone with Dyta.'

Auntie Mary appeared uncomfortable, and did not ask why. Neither did I tell her, but I had the feeling that she knew more than she was prepared to admit.

She kissed me without saying a word, and away she went on her bike.

I entered the house quietly. Luckily the bedroom door was closed. I went to the back kitchen, stripped naked, and washed myself carefully all over in cold water and carbolic soap. I then put on clean clothes, and plaited my hair. I felt I had to cleanse myself thoroughly in order to get rid of all traces of the Master's dirty paws.

21

I had to pretend that I was sick – very sick. So I went out to the garden to practise. I started off with sneezing, followed by coughing, and a general weakness of the limbs, because it was vital to persuade Mamo that I would be quite unfit to attend school the following day.

A big, purple bruise had appeared on my neck, the result of the Master's madness. I covered that up by winding my stocking around it: that was a certain cure for a sore throat too, especially if steeped in camphorated oil. I found a bottle of that in the outside kitchen. I was quite determined – I was *not* going to attend school the following day, come what may. I was fortunate that the morrow was a Friday, then I would have Saturday and Sunday to work out my plan of action for the coming week.

Mamo hardly took notice of my illness – she was really and truly sick, almost too weak to talk. It was one of her bad days. Poor Mamo.

Friday was Marged's day. To deceive her would be no problem. Her strength, or maybe her weakness, was to believe everybody and to trust every scamp. She spoilt me from my cradle days, and but for Marged's love and mollycoddling I would have had a very unhappy babyhood. But strangely I could never open my heart to her as I did to Auntie Mary. She fussed over me all day, believed all I said, and prepared enough cawl and rice pudding to last over the weekend.

Dyta arrived home on his rickety bike. Apparently he was tricked when he bought his motor-bike, and that had upset him. So he condemned the seller to hell for ever, and that most eloquently. His greatest worry was that he had to continue to pay his half-a-crown weekly for his dead bike.

I had to carry on sneezing, coughing and spitting without respite. I was quite pleased with myself – I managed to deceive everybody, including Sara and Mari. Mari gave me some sickly medicine to take – I poured it all out into the garden, hoping that it would not poison the birds.

But the lump of disgust remained solid in my stomach, with the shame of having to face the Master again, exactly as if I were to blame. But it was his fault and his shame, or Auntie Mary would never have called him a devil.

What possessed the Master, and Dyta too, to abuse a child like me? Did other children have to suffer the same fate? If not, why me? We all knew that the Master liked to tickle the big girls, but what I had to suffer was different. He wasn't the Master, but a madman, and he didn't care how badly he hurt me. I just could not forget the disgust; it had penetrated too deeply. I went over the incident over and over again, but could make no sense at all of it. Why? Why me?

Nor did I go to school on Monday – I kept suffering from the cold! But who should call on Monday evening but Miss Evans. Luckily Mamo was in bed, and that saved a great deal of questioning and explaining.

'I have brought you your coat, cap and school bag.'

'Thank you, Miss Evans.'

The stocking still remained around my neck, and I coughed loudly to prove the point.

Miss Evans took no notice and there was silence – dead silence.

She too seemed to be lost for words.

'How's your mother, Jini.'

'Just the same, no better, Miss Evans.'

I had given up telling people that she was on the mend. Suddenly, maybe due to the sympathy in Miss Evans's voice, but also due to Mamo's illness and my uncertain future, but above all because of the Master's insanity, because of all my sorrows, I burst out crying uncontrollably. Miss Evans embraced me lovingly, and there were tears in her eyes too. I could feel her affection, and I knew that her sympathy was genuine. We stood clasped for some time and then she said, 'You will come to school tomorrow, Jini?'

It was obvious that she had seen through my 'bad cold'. Perhaps Auntie Mary had been carrying tales.

'I don't know.'

'What about the Scholarship, Jini?'

I was stumped. Should I tell her the truth, the whole truth?

Before I had time to reply, she said, 'Listen Jini my love, listen carefully. You will regret it all your life if you don't carry on with your education. You are an outstanding scholar Jini, you are the brightest pupil I've ever had the privilege of teaching. Education is all-important: you can never be independent and be mistress of your own destiny unless you have the necessary qualifications.'

I had to agree with her. There was complete silence for a minute or so. She then placed her hands on my shoulders and looked into the very depths of my eyes.

'Jini, listen, and I mean what I say. What happened to you last Thursday afternoon in school will never, never happen to you again. I swear to you on God's word.'

I then realised that she knew the whole dirty story – Auntie Mary must have told her everything. Miss Evans knew the Master better than anyone and I felt that with her at my side, I need not be afraid ever again.

'Jini, will you come to school tomorrow?'

'Yes, Miss Evans.'

We embraced once more, and I was neither afraid nor ashamed to face the Master on the following day.

I did go to school as I had promised – late – on purpose. I felt shaky and nervous. I discarded the stocking and the bruise had spread. It was very much in evidence. If someone was to ask me how it had happened, I would just tell them that I had slipped and knocked myself against a chair. And yet, I was anxious that the Master should notice it, knowing full well that he would not dare ask for an explanation. As I passed Miss Evans's class, she smiled and gave me a sly wink. I went out to play at 'small playtime', also during the dinner hour, and left Johnnie on his own to study for the Scholarship. When it came to 'stay behind', the Master for the first time that day gave me a look, and a nasty look it was too. I looked at him straight in the eye and said haughtily, 'I can't stay behind, I must go home early. My mother is ill.'

I knew instinctively that I was the boss now, and that he would never, never abuse me again.

At heart he was a coward, an old bully. I would never be afraid of him again.

There was only another month before the Scholarship, and I felt that I knew enough to pass without the extra lessons. For weeks now we hadn't learnt anything new – we only went over the same old stuff – the same essays, the same sums and the same grammar rules. I was really and truly fed up.

When I arrived home, my mother was up and about, and to my surprise, tea was laid on the table. I felt elated, maybe she was only suffering from a bad cold, after all. After tea, she led me into the parlour, took a key from her pocket and opened the bottom drawer of the 'chest and drawers'. I had a shock. The drawer was full of treasures – gold watches, rings, chains, necklaces and brooches of every description.

'Mamo, where did all these come from? It is like the fairies' treasure trove.'

'They are mine, Jini.'

'Yours? Where did you find them?'

'Some belonged to my grandmother, others belonged to my mother, but most of them were presents given to me by my father.'

'They are worth a fortune, Mamo. You are a rich woman.'

'After I am gone, they will be yours; I want you to cherish them and guard them, and when you are grown up you will be able to wear them. But if ever you will need money to pay for your education you are welcome to sell them. But never sell them unless it is absolutely necessary.'

'But Mamo, who was . . . ?'

'Please Jini, don't ask me any more questions. But I want you to make a solemn promise – an oath. I want you to promise with your right hand on the Bible that you will go to the County School and afterwards to College. Grow up to be independent, Jini, and never, never depend on your father. He is not to be trusted.'

She then fetched the English Bible. I had to place my right hand on it and repeat after her, 'I swear on my word of honour, that I shall attend the County School, and afterwards attend College in order to graduate, so that I shall be independent and be my own mistress. So help me God.'

Apparently, if you place your hand on the Bible, and swear solemnly, that promise will be sacred and lasting. And if that promise is ever broken you will have sinned unforgivably not only against your family but against God himself. That is what Mamo said. But I could not possibly believe how putting one's hand on the Bible could make it so binding.

We supped together. I felt very close to her, and I realised that I loved Mamo above everyone and everything. Even above God himself.

I tried to find out more about my grandparents, but instead of answering me, she started to cry – a desperate cry that she could not control. That started off the cough. She coughed and heaved all through the night, and by morning she was too weak to talk. The decline had returned with a vengeance and was determined to take its toll.

22

The day of reckoning arrived and for the first time in more than a month, the Master deigned to talk to me – very reluctantly. I was told that a car would be waiting for me outside Morgan's Shop at nine o'clock on Saturday morning.

I got up early and prepared breakfast for myself and Mamo. She was almost too weak to sit up in bed and hardly touched her breakfast. But she wished me well and said in a whisper, 'Do your very best, Jini *fach*. It is of the utmost importance that you pass. Good luck, *cariad*.'

I left in good time, but when I arrived, there was no one in sight – no car, no Johnnie, and no Master.

The postman came.

'What time is it please.'

'If you are waiting for the car, that's gone. It went half an hour ago.'

'Has Johnnie gone?'

'Yes, so has the Master, and the Mistress, too.'

I was very upset. Mr Morgan the Shop arrived on the scene and he realised that something was wrong.

'Jini *fach*, the car left half an hour ago.'

'I was told to meet the car at nine o'clock.'

'Today is Scholarship day, isn't it?'

'What shall I do, Mr Morgan?'

'Jini,' he said, 'would you be prepared to ride pillion on my motor-bike?'

I thanked him profusely. I would be prepared to ride pillion on an elephant provided I could arrive at the County School in time.

'Right,' he said, 'put your arms round my waist, hold tight, and don't look at the hedges.'

Away we went. I clasped him tightly; my hair flying in the wind – the buckle that held it neatly together blew away and was lost. But no matter, I arrived at the school gates, dishevelled but safely. I walked in nervously through the huge oak door and I could see through another door, a glass door, rows and rows of children with their heads down writing furiously. I knocked timidly on the door, and a tall man wearing a black gown and a square flat cap answered.

'Yes, and what do you want, child?'

'I have come to sit the Scholarship, Sir. Sorry to be late.'

'What is your name?'

'Mary Anne Jane John, Sir.'

He disappeared, but returned in a few minutes – minutes that seemed more like hours. 'Where is your pen and ruler, girl?' Nobody had told me that I needed a pen and a ruler.

At long last I was provided with the necessary tools, plus a blotting paper. I felt dreadful, everybody was busy writing, and I was sure I would never to be able to catch up with them. I saw Johnnie in the distance, but he didn't even glance at me. I felt lonely and neglected. Why did the Master deceive me? Why did he say nine o'clock when the car was due at half past eight? Was it a genuine mistake, or was it spite? Was it his sly way of wreaking his vengeance? Was he punishing me for telling Auntie Mary, and she in turn telling Miss Evans? That made me more determined than ever to do my very best. To hell with the Master – using Dyta's language gave me courage in a crisis.

The questions were not difficult, but because I was late I couldn't finish the paper.

At twelve o'clock we had a break to refresh ourselves. Everyone had brought a packed lunch – everyone except me. They all carried cups too – everyone except me. Johnnie took pity on me and shared his bread-and-butter and jam sandwiches with me. I was famished. Good old Johnnie. The school cook brewed the tea, and she very kindly lent me a cup. The Master had told Johnnie precisely what to do, and what to bring along, and that the taxi would be waiting for us at eight-thirty prompt.

Johnnie also told me about the arrangements for going home – the car would be at the school gates waiting for him at four o'clock. So I made up my mind to stick to Johnnie like a leech, and ride home in style in the car.

'There is something very odd about the Master lately. He says the strangest things, Jini. He said that you were a hussy. What's a hussy, Jini?'

'You had better ask him, Johnnie.'

'He also said that you were a liar and never to be trusted. Is that true, Jini?'

'Of course not. He is the one you can't trust. The bloody fool. The man is on his way to the mad-house in Carmarthen, and but for Morgan the Shop I would still be waiting for the taxi.'

'You are a funny bird, Jini. You don't care two hoots about him, do you?'

'No I don't, Johnnie. He is an old devil and if I fail the Scholarship, it will be his fault and his only.'

Before I had the chance to call him any more names, the car arrived. The Master sat looking sullenly next to the driver. He appeared quite surprised when he saw me, but I didn't care. Mrs Master sat like a duchess on the back seat. She was wearing a huge black hat, and a feather boa around her shoulders. I pushed myself in and sat next to her. She didn't shift her big body an inch to the side. Neither did she glance at us. Johnnie followed and no one said a word. Not a word about the exam, and no one asked how I had arrived that morning. Not one word was said during the whole journey. Johnnie and I alighted at the school house.

'Thank you,' said Johnnie politely. I kept my mouth shut tightly. As far as I was concerned, they didn't deserve thanks.

When I arrived home, Dr Powell was at the house and he and Dyta were whispering in the back kitchen. My heart sank. Dr Powell turned to me and said slowly and sadly, 'Listen to me, *cariad*. It's not right that you should sleep in the same room as your mother.'

'Why not, doctor?'

'She needs peace and rest to recuperate.'

'But I am perfectly quiet. And what's more, she needs someone at hand to provide her with a hot drink at night. Her cough is terrible at night.'

Dr Powell and Dyta looked at each other – the type of look that speaks without words. Eventually the doctor said, 'Jini, I'm sorry to have to tell you, but your mother is suffering from the decline, and the decline is an evil disease. It is very catching.'

'I know that, Dr Powell. I've known it for a long time. I'm not afraid of the decline, and what's more, somebody must care for her. There is no one else. But if you insist, I'm prepared to sleep on the sofa in the kitchen.'

Dr Powell looked long and hard at Dyta, but Dyta looked down at his boots and said not a word.

When I told Mamo of the new arrangements she found the strength to sit up in bed, her eyes flaming, and said quite clearly, with anger in her voice, 'You are *not* to sleep in the kitchen, not on any account. Do you hear? Do you promise?'

'Yes Mamo, I promise.'

She then slumped back on the pillows and said in a whisper, 'Perhaps Sara and Mari will allow you to sleep at Glan-dŵr.'

I knew full well why she wouldn't allow me to sleep in the kitchen. She didn't trust Dyta. Neither did I. But I could not possibly leave her on her own. So when Auntie Mary arrived, I told her the whole story, and she in her wisdom drew out a rota of those who were to look after Mamo at night. I would be at home to care for her during the day. I had stopped going to school now the Scholarship was over.

According to Auntie Mary's list, Dyta was to come home and watch over Mamo every Saturday night and every Sunday night. Auntie Mary on Mondays and Fridays, Sara on Tuesday and Mari on Wednesdays and Thursdays.

The put-you-up canvas bed was taken down to Glan-dŵr, and I slept there in the kitchen every night. It was a dreadful, wearisome time.

All hope had vanished. Dr Powell himself had pronounced the word clearly and emphatically. Mamo was suffering from the decline, and nobody, not even God himself, could cure the decline.

During the long nights on my uncomfortable canvas bed I would toss and turn and worry about the future. What would become of me? I was worried. So I determined to accept each day as it came, and to try to keep smiling for Mamo's sake.

I stayed away from school most of the time. Sometimes Sara would come and relieve me. Marged and her basket turned up every Friday without fail. Thanks be to God for Marged. The Master was absent too – it was said he'd had a stroke. I didn't care – the school was a healthier place without him.

Miss Evans was in charge of the top class, until a certain Miss Rees arrived to relieve her. She was a newly qualified teacher. A big, hefty girl with ginger hair, cropped like a man's; she carried a cane in her hand all day long and slapped the desks with it. I am certain the school would have been a quieter and better run place without her. It was hullabaloo – fun-and-games, and disobedience. But for Miss Evans it would have been rebellion. I failed to join in the tomfoolery. I was so upset about Mamo, and about my future too. Her illness was like a black cloud hovering over my life. I was also worked up about the Scholarship. To fail would have killed Mamo sooner than the decline would have done. I prayed every night – prayed that I would pass. It would have been no use whatsoever to pray for Mamo's recovery – Mamo was beyond all help. Both God and Dr Powell had given her up.

One night, when I was alone with Mamo, thinking that all the world was against me, there was a knock at the door. It was Miss Evans. Surprise, surprise! I was so pleased to see her.

Her very first words were, 'Congrats, Jini, you've passed. The third on the list.'

'And Johnnie?'

'He was first – top of the list.'

I didn't stop to talk. I didn't even thank her. I rushed to the bedroom and shouted, 'Mamo, Mamo, I've passed the Scholarship. Third from the top, Mamo.'

She found the strength to half sit up in bed, and said quite clearly, 'Thanks be to God.' She then fell back on the pillows and smiled at me – a beautiful smile. I too thanked God. She had found at least one reason to smile about. I kissed her gently on the forehead. There was no need for words.

I closed the bedroom door quietly. I asked Miss Evans inside – she was standing patiently on the doorstep. I told her the whole story – how I was stranded in the village, the mad ride on the motor-bike, arriving late, and not being able to finish all the questions.

'What a tale of adventure, Jini. There were only three marks between you and Johnnie, and if you'd had time to finish, you would have been top.' She kissed me and congratulated me again.

For the first time in many months, I felt it was worthwhile to be alive. But my joy did not last long. The cloud of doom returned and Miss Evans was quick to notice.

'What is wrong, Jini? Why the sad look?'

'Mamo is going to die soon, and then my home will be gone.'

'Don't lose hope, Jini. If the worst comes to the worst, you will always have your father to look after you.'

'I can never live in the same house as my father.'

'Why, Jini?'

'I can't explain, Miss Evans, that wouldn't be fair to Dyta.'

'No, of course not. I should not have asked. But I promise you, Jini, on my word of honour, that I shall do all I can to help you. It would be a sin if a bright girl like you missed her chance in life.'

Miss Evans was a lovely person and I loved

her dearly. I felt better and more cheerful than I had felt for a long time.

But that mood did not remain for long. My heart sank when I spied Dyta and his bike arriving. Why come home tonight? It was Auntie Mary's turn to watch over Mamo.

Miss Evans greeted him amiably. 'Good evening, Mr John' – but he didn't have the good manners to reply.

Miss Evans then left abruptly, and I rushed to tell Dyta the good news. 'I've passed, Dyta.'

No reply.

'But Dyta, I've passed the Scholarship. I've passed to go to the County School.'

'I 'eard. And who do you think is going to pay for you milady to go to that place? Me? Not bloody likely.'

'But Dyta, nobody needs to pay. Passing the Scholarship means school for free.'

'Jini, if you believe that, you're a bloody fool. Who will pay your lodgings? Who, I'd like to know? And what about books and clothes? I have no money to throw away to keep you like a bloomin' stuck up lady. No bloody fear.'

I ran outside. I just couldn't listen to him. It was the stark truth of course. Who would pay? There was nobody but Dyta. I couldn't stop the tears. Dyta followed me out and put his arms lovingly around me, and said, 'Don't cry, Jini *fach*. Forget about the County School. Us two will be 'appy together at Llety'r Wennol. 'Appy like two young doves.'

I stood quite still. I was too petrified to move and an icy shiver ran up and down my spine. He took it for granted that Mamo would soon be dead. At that moment hatred possessed me, hatred towards Dyta, and I could think of no worse punishment than having to live under the same roof as my father. Just the two of us. It terrified me.

I shrugged myself free of him. There was so much to do – bed-changing, washing, mangling, ironing – non-stop.

The mangle was so big and cumbersome, it was a struggle to turn the handle. So off I went out of Dyta's sight to mangle – that gigantic wooden contraption which gave out a doleful squeal every time I turned the handle. It was a pitiful sound which echoed my troubled thoughts. And I just could not stop crying – however hard I tried.

I went to the garden at the back of the house to hang out the clothes; suddenly from behind two rough hands covered my eyes.

'Guess who?'

Dyta of course, and before I realised what was happening I was flat on my back on the ground with Dyta on top of me.

'Jini *fach*, you be a good girl, 'cos Dyta loves you. Don't shout or struggle, and you'll be fine.'

But I did shout and I did struggle. At that he covered my mouth with his mighty hand and that stifled every sound and shout. He lifted up my clothes, stripped me of my bloomers, and half stripped himself. He pushed and he thrust and he shoved while I lay on my back helpless, without force or energy. He hurt me terribly, but I could neither scream nor cry. I didn't know how long I suffered – ten minutes, twenty minutes, maybe more. I was petrified, time did not exist. I was certain I was going to die. I ached all over.

Then suddenly I heard a voice in the distance, 'Jini, where are you?'

Dyta got up hastily, jumped over the hedge like a wild beast, dragging his trousers after him. Auntie Mary shouted again. I answered feebly. She came and saw my half naked condition.

'Jini. Who Jini? For God's sake, who?'

'Dyta.'

'God help us!'

She stooped down and embraced me as we lay together on the grass in complete silence; both of us conscious of the shame and disgust. There was no need for words – our tears spoke for us.

23

We hugged each other, lying there on the cold earth, Auntie Mary comforting me tearfully.

'You wait – when I get hold of Ifan John I shall make him regret that he was ever born. He will never be able to forget what he did to you today. The rascal.'

We both agreed not to tell Mamo. So Auntie Mary went into the house quietly by way of the front door and I entered by the back door.

I stripped completely and scrubbed my body all over using carbolic soap. I felt dirty and soiled, as if the Devil himself had tortured me. And that very Devil was Dyta himself, so that made me Satan's child. Horrible thought.

Relationships sometimes can bring disgrace and shame to your nearest and dearest. Why? Why did he behave like a beast? And why did Mamo marry such a blackguard? She who is such a fine lady. Why?

The bedroom door was open wide, and I could hear voices. At least I could hear what Auntie Mary said, but Mamo's voice was too feeble. I could not catch one word of what she said.

'. . .'

'Jini is washing in the back kitchen.'

'. . .'

'No, I didn't see Ifan.'

'. . .'

'Don't worry, Myfi darling. I promise on oath that I shall take care of Jini.'

'. . .'

'Myfi, my dear, you will get better again. You must have faith.'

'. . .'

'Myfi, you must believe me. I shall look after Jini. I will see that she attends the County School. Yes, and College too. I promise you, on my word of honour, that she will come to no harm.'

'. . .'

'No, I shall ignore Ifan. He will not be allowed to look after her. I promise.'

They closed the door and I heard no more.

It was obvious that Mamo was losing ground and growing weaker by the minute. I would have to be of good courage. I found myself more worried about myself than I was of Mamo. She was dying and beyond help. But what would become of me?

'Jini will come to no harm'. What did that mean? She didn't say that I could go and live with her. Pen-gwern was a big house, and apart from her, her father, and two maids, no one else lived there.

Mari used to say that God always took care

of all orphans, but according to the Bible one had to die before you could live in heaven, which is God's house.

I went to Mamo's room to bid her goodnight. It was Auntie Mary's turn to 'keep watch' and she was with her, sitting quietly, holding her hand. Mamo had a strange look about her, her skin was like alabaster, and her big blue eyes appeared wild and restless. She had a far-away look on her face, and I felt uncomfortable. She raised her hand and I kissed it. She whispered, 'Good night, Jini my darling. Be a good girl. *Always.*'

Auntie Mary accompanied me to the gate.

'Mamo is very ill tonight.'

'Yes Jini, very ill. I'll stay here with you tomorrow.'

'She's dying, isn't she?'

'I'm afraid so, Jini. We must be brave and submit to divine providence.'

'Providence? What providence? Who would want Mamo to die?'

'I cannot answer that question, Jini, I can only hope that she will find more joy in that other world than she has found in this world.'

'It is all Dyta's fault. Why did she marry such a good-for-nothing lout?'

'Nor can I answer that question, Jini.'

It was clear that she didn't want to answer.

'Goodnight Jini dear, come back early in the morning. I need you here.'

And away I went to Glan-dŵr to sleep on my narrow canvas bed. I could not sleep. I tossed and turned. My body ached and my thoughts were disturbed and confused. I cursed Dyta, I wept for Mamo, and pitied myself. I tried to pray too, prayed that somebody, somewhere would take pity on me, and that I would find a home, so that I could attend the County School.

There was no point in praying for Mamo – she was beyond all help, and I didn't want to waste Jesus Christ's precious time. As for Dyta, he didn't deserve anybody's prayers – he was the devil's kinsman. It was partly because of him that I couldn't sleep. I was badly injured, bruised all over, and sick at heart.

Was I different from every other girl? Or did all girls have to suffer as I did in order to grow into womanhood? If so, why was Auntie Mary so angry and disgusted? Why?

However, after caring for Mamo, knowing that she woud never get better, and the nasty revolting incidents with the Master and Dyta, I felt that I was a child no longer. So I determined to act and behave like a mature woman, and not to depend so much on Auntie Mary, Sara and Mari.

I got up early. I hadn't slept a wink – worry and pain had kept me awake. I rushed up to Llety'r Wennol and found Auntie Mary washing and changing Mamo.

She was too weak to sit up in bed, and she couldn't even whisper, but she managed a faint smile. Auntie Mary was silent; she just gave me one look, and that look spoke for itself. I couldn't stay in the room. I couldn't bear to see her broken body. It wasn't Mamo's body, it was merely a body that had lost the will to live.

I busied to prepare breakfast, but neither of us ate anything. We only drank tea. Mamo now could not swallow anything, not even a sip of water. In order to allay the tumult in my brain, I set about cleaning the house – washing the floor, scrubbing the kitchen table, cleaning windows, and giving the furniture in Mamo's room an extra polish. The bedroom furniture was of mahogany and so beautiful – quite different from the other bits and pieces in the house. Mamo took no notice of me. I clasped her hand gently and kissed it. No response. Was she dying? Was this how people died?

Dyta had disappeared, much to Auntie Mary's disappointment. She was ready for him – in order 'to make him regret that he had ever been born'.

Dr Powell called around midday. He said nothing – shook his head. That was all.

'Dr Powell,' I said, talking like a grown-up, and not as a child. 'Why didn't you send Mamo to hospital? Jack Tŷ-draw was sent to Llanybydder for treatment, and they say he is getting better, and that he will be home soon.'

'Jini, my dear, your mother was in an advanced stage of the sickness when I first saw her, and we must catch that terrible disease right at the beginning, or God help us. But, we doctors are learning all the time, and before long I am sure we shall even conquer the decline.'

'That is of no comfort to us, Dr Powell. Mamo is on the point of dying, isn't she?'

'Yes, I'm afraid so, Jini *fach*. You are a very brave girl. Your father and your Auntie Mary, I'm certain, will take care of you.'

'I can take care of myself, Dr Powell.'

He ignored my assertion, and after a short while said, 'Your father should be here, Jini, you should send for him.'

Dyta was the very last person I wanted to see. I hadn't seen him since that horrible business in the garden when he vanished like a hunted fox over the garden hedge. When Auntie Mary and I returned to the house, the bike and its owner had disappeared. And we were glad.

The doctor prepared to leave. He took another peep at Mamo – just a peep, no more. There was nothing he could do. Auntie Mary sat at her bedside holding her hand, moving only to wipe the sweat from her forehead. Mari arrived. Faithful old Mari, fussing around, eager to help.

'Ifan should be here. I shall send Sara to the Post tomorrow to send him a wire. No, on second thoughts, I'll go home and tell her to go at once.'

I stayed with Auntie Mary and Mamo. I stood on one side holding Mamo's left hand and Auntie Mary on the other side holding her other hand, exactly as if we were keeping her back from death. It was a fearful, unreal situation. We could hardly hear her breathing. We stayed in that position for a long, long time – for an hour, or maybe two or three hours. Time did not exist.

Then suddenly she gave a long, loud breath, and stopped. That was the moment when the spirit departed from her body. The spirit that was such a mystery to me. Mamo was dead.

Auntie Mary let go of her hand and kissed her on the forehead. I did the same.

The top white sheet was pulled up to cover her face, and we left her alone and lonely. No one could help her any more. Mamo had died peacefully after years of suffering, leaving me forsaken and homeless.

We went to the kitchen quietly, on tiptoe, exactly as if we were afraid to disturb the invisible being. We drank tea in silence, we drank the teapot dry. Everything had been said. It was as if time had stood still, with no hope for the future.

Mari arrived, with details of the 'wire' and the peace was shattered.

'She has passed away, Mari, and we must carry out the last office.'

'What do you mean, Auntie Mary?'

'We must dress her for the coffin. Mari will do what is necessary and I shall be there to help.'

I stayed in the kitchen, hearing doors and drawers being opened and closed. Why prepare her for the grave? She would be hidden away, deep down in the cold earth. I was stunned; my tongue was parched, the tears had dried up, my eyes were scorching, and I felt an emptiness inside me.

After a long, long time, Auntie Mary entered the kitchen.

'Jini, we have finished. Would you like to see your mother now?'

'If you wish me to come, I will do so. But Mamo has gone, it is only an empty body that is left.'

But when the cover was withdrawn I had a shock. There lay the most beautiful woman I had ever seen. Her eyes were closed and she appeared to be asleep. Her shining black hair fell over her shoulders and framed her face. She was dressed in a bright blue silk dress – a dress which had been hidden, hanging in the big wardrobe over the years. Never in my life had I seen anyone so lovely, so serene.

Yes, definitely, she was Mamo, my very own mother – my darling mother who had escaped from her affliction and torment, and yes, from her husband too.

24

Dyta did not arrive home that day. Nor the day after that. Mari blamed Morgan the Post for his carelessness.

'But never mind,' said Mari, 'I shall stay tonight, although it is the proper thing that the nearest relative should stay guard on the first night-watch.'

'Watch? Watch what? Mamo is dead, no one can do anything for her anymore.'

'You don't understand, Jini – no one knows what time exactly the spirit departs from the body, and it is of the utmost importance that the body should be watched over, tonight of all nights. I hope your father will return for tomorrow's watch.'

And I was under the impression that Mamo's spirit had departed the moment she died.

'Mari, what is this spirit you keep on about? I thought the spirit and the soul were one and the same.'

'Only the Parson can answer such questions, Jini. You must ask him.

Avoiding the issue as always. And I thought that Mari knew her Bible.

Auntie Mary had gone. She had left on her bike to see Marged, the Rector, and John Saer the carpenter, to make the arrangements for the funeral. She would call back later that evening to take me to Pen-gwern.

Apparently, we would have to go shopping; I would have to buy a new rig-out – mourning clothes in order to show respect for the dead. I just couldn't fathom how wearing black clothes could make any difference to the respect I had for Mamo.

John Saer arrived to 'measure' Mamo so that the coffin should fit her perfectly, and turned to Mari, who was 'on watch'.

'I suppose they will want the best oak for the coffin, and also the finest trimmings?'

'Does it matter with what sort of trimmings you will decorate the coffin? They will only be buried out of sight in the ground,' said I, speaking as if I were an expert on coffins and trimmings.

'Jini!' said Mari in a reproachful voice, 'remember it is your good mother who will lie in that coffin.'

John went into the bedroom to 'measure', and when he came out there was a tiny tear lurking in the corner of his eye, and in a trembling voice said, 'I have never seen a more beautiful corpse laid out and prepared for any coffin.'

Seeing John Saer grieving for Mamo made me realise anew the cruelty of losing my nearest and dearest. She was my only relative. Dyta was no longer related to me; no decent father would abuse his little girl the way Dyta had abused me. Shame upon him.

I went out to the garden, out of everybody's sight and wept – wept piteously. I wept because Mamo had died. I wept because Dyta was such a brute and I wept for myself, because I was now a homeless orphan.

Later, Auntie Mary returned, not on her bike, but in a posh new motor car. I knew her father had bought a car, but I didn't know that she could drive. So off we went in style to Pen-gwern, leaving Mari to 'keep watch' over the dead.

I felt uncomfortable and sad leaving Mamo, even though she was dead. Maybe her spirit was still hovering around.

But Auntie Mary was quite determined. I was to go shopping for mourning clothes. I would be allowed to go home for the funeral, but that would not take place for another four days.

So off we went, Auntie Mary and myself, to buy deep black, mourning clothes, and also a silly hat which perched at an angle on my head – not unlike a Jim Crow hat. I felt a real fool. I had no interest in my new mourning clothes. None whatsoever.

By the end of the day, *hiraeth* possessed me. I longed to return to Llety'r Wennol to have one peep at Mamo, before they finally put the lid on the coffin. Auntie Mary drove me home the following day – not in the posh car, but in a horse and trap. Leaning against the wall were two bikes. One was Dyta's ramshackle machine; the other looked a little bit more respectable.

Dyta had arrived. He was accompanied by a big pot-bellied man, taller even than Dyta, but with the same colour hair – bright ginger. They were both in their working clothes – wearing 'yorks', red kerchiefs, and heavy hobnailed boots. They were not a pretty sight. The stranger was Dyta's brother. Their story was that they had rushed here the minute they had received the wire; hoping to see her before she died. The big brother was the speaker. Dyta sat in the most comfortable chair, looked at the floor and snuffled into a dirty handkerchief. Marged, Mari and Sara joined in the snuffling. Dyta was determined not to look up and we both knew why. There was silence for a while and then the big brother said, 'She looks very nice in her coffin.'

Nice! Nice? Yes, that is what the old fool said. I was shaken and dumbfounded. I realised then that the coffin had arrived while I was gallivanting around the shops, and I had a dreadful feeling that I had shirked my responsibilities. I shouldn't have left Mamo in the care of strangers. I should have stayed with her until the very end. And that end would not come until the soil had completely covered her coffin in the graveyard.

I entered the bedroom on tiptoe and bolted the door. I wanted to ask her forgiveness, because by now I half believed Mari's story about the spirit and that it might still be hovering around. I gazed at her in wonder, amazed at her beauty and the peaceful look on her face. I caught hold of her hand, but I withdrew it quickly. It was like clutching a piece of marble. Someone rattled the door, but the bolt was firm and steady. I needed time to chat to Mamo on my own, without interference. I wanted to tell her that I would always behave myself, for her sake, and that I would go to the County School, come what may, and that too for her sake. I didn't mention Dyta and his misdeeds, she knew him better than anyone, or she would never have asked Auntie Mary to be my guardian.

Talking, promising and bending over the coffin caused me to break down completely. I had no control over my tears. It was a relief, and I felt nearer to that corpse in the coffin than I had felt to Mamo when she was alive. I felt a wave of affection flowing through me and I promised on oath whilst gazing at the dead, motionless face, that from that day onwards I would try to please her above all else. I would never obey or listen to Dyta ever again. Never, no more. From that day forward I was determined to be the mistress of my own destiny.

The door rattled again. 'Are you all right, Jini dear? Come, it's time to go home.'

As I bade Mamo farewell, I felt calmer and more at ease, and hearing Auntie Mary saying 'time to go home' gave me a feeling of belonging and stability. No, I would never be homeless whilst Auntie Mary remained alive. I felt very sad having to leave Mamo all alone in her coffin, but she was beyond all sorrow and pain, and no living person could ever hurt her again.

As we were about to depart, Dyta asked in a put-on trembling voice, 'When is the funeral? I want to order a glass wreath from Jini and me.'

Before anyone had a chance to reply, I blurted out, 'You please yourself about a wreath, but don't include me in your plans. I shall buy my own flowers to put on Mamo's grave.'

Auntie Mary then had her say. 'Jini can well look after herself if left alone. The funeral is on Wednesday, eleven o'clock at the house. Remember to attend on time, so that you can assist in carrying the coffin shoulder high. It will be your last chance to show her any respect. She deserves that, after all she's had to suffer throughout the years.'

'Hold on, hold on,' said big brother. 'Ifan thought the world of his wife.'

Auntie Mary merely snorted and ignored him. 'I'll have a word with you, Ifan, after the funeral. We have a lot to talk about, haven't we?'

Dyta made no reply, and carried on examining his boots. He didn't even have the courtesy to get up to bid us farewell, and he was lucky that there were others present or Auntie Mary would have jumped down his throat and 'made him sorry that he had ever been born'.

Auntie Mary had not forgotten her promise; she was merely biding her time, and I wouldn't like to be in Dyta's boots when that hour came.

I felt easier in my mind after having that chat with Mamo, and I half believed that Mamo's spirit could still be wandering around until the coffin was finally closed.

I felt glad to escape from Dyta and his big, unshaven brother, and to return to the comfort of Pen-gwern. I was waiting anxiously for Auntie Mary to declare once and for all, that Pen-gwern would be my future home. But to my disappointment, nothing was said.

I spent the following day very quietly – remembering, grieving, and trying to solve the problem of the soul and the spirit. Were they one and the same? The resurrection too? How could the bodies which had been buried deep down in the earth, most of them for centuries, arise and ascend to heaven? I would have to listen carefully to the Parson during the church service, to see if I could find any sort of explanation for the mystery.

The service would be in English, but no matter, I could understand both languages equally, and concentrating on the Rector's words would stop me from imagining Mamo lying in that coffin. I was determined not to cry; not in front of the people present. I would have to be strong and hold back my tears. Dr Powell told me to be brave; it would not be easy, but I was determined to follow his advice. I would have to try and forget that it was my mother who was lying dead inside that coffin, screwed down tightly, for ever and ever. Amen.

21

Wednesday. The first Wednesday in the month of August, nineteen hundred and twenty five.

That was the day we were to bury Mamo.

I got up early, around six o'clock. I hadn't slept a wink all night. I ate no breakfast and I dressed in my funeral, deep-mourning clothes, cross-grained and grudgingly. I refused to put on my Jim Crow hat.

It was raining; not heavily, just a drizzle. Mr Puw had promised to drive Auntie Mary and myself to Llety'r Wennol in time for the service. Mr Puw's car was an open tourer, with a hood attached, but in spite of much heaving and pushing, the hood refused to function, with the result that we had to open our umbrellas whilst travelling. Sara and Mari were there to greet us, both wearing deep black from top to toe.

It is strange how I still remember vividly every tiny detail of what happened that grief-stricken morning.

Dyta had not returned from Pembrokeshire, where he had gone back to fetch his funeral clothes. Sara and Mari had prepared enough food to feed the whole parish – bread-and-butter (thinly sliced), jam, cheese and currant loaf.

The coffin had not been closed, so I entered the bedroom on tiptoe, in case I disturbed the spirit. But I had the feeling that it had now departed, and that there was nothing left anymore – just a dead body. I now believed that Mari was right about the spirit – it had now escaped and left an empty carcass. Maybe Dyta had frightened him; he was the type of man who was capable of driving away every spirit and saint.

Dyta and his brother arrived, well turned-out in deep mourning and wearing bowler hats. Dyta's hat was too big, but fortunately his ears were also big and able to support the hat. They had arrived in a hired car, driven by a nondescript little man wearing a cloth cap. They ate ravenously, all three, and cleared a fair amount of the food. But in fairness, they behaved well, and I heard no swear words, not even the ever-present 'bloody'. It must have been a mighty effort for Dyta to choose his words so carefully.

Then John Saer and the hearse arrived, drawn by a beautiful white horse. John entered the bedroom, head bent, and asked almost in a whisper, 'Would you like to see the body before I close the coffin?'

They all traipsed in – all except me. I didn't want to see the body – it wasn't Mamo anymore, and moreover it would annoy me to watch Dyta and his brother practising hypocrisy, snuffling dry-eyed into their new white handerkerchiefs edged with black. I made an excuse that I needed to go outside to the 'small house'. I stayed there until I was quite certain that the lid of the coffin had been screwed down, shutting Mamo away from us for ever. I hadn't forgotten the horrible scratching and screeching when John Saer screwed the lid on my little brother's coffin.

Just before eleven the Rector arrived in his brand new car. He shook hands ceremoniously with all present, and sympathised with Dyta and myself. He spoke English with a twang, knowing full well that we were all of us Welsh, and spoke nothing but Welsh. We all pushed into the bedroom. It was a tight fit, because the coffin occupied most of the space.

He commenced the service in a high-pitched monotonous voice.

'The Lord be with you, and with Thy spirit,
The Lord have mercy upon us,
Christ have mercy upon us.'
Then he said, 'Let us pray together.'
'Our Father, which art in Heaven
Hallowed by thy name . . .'
But only Auntie Mary and her father responded, no one else knew the English version of the Lord's prayer.

Then away the Rector went amidst a cloud of smoke that belched from underneath his car.

Dyta, his brother, Mr Puw and John Saer carried the coffin to the hearse.

To my surprise, Dyta turned to me and said in a subdued, gentle voice, his funeral voice, 'Jini, *cariad*, you had best ride with me and your Uncle Jim in our car, because you and me are the chief mourners, and us should be following the coffin.'

That is when I noticed the black ribbons tied around the lamps of the car.

Before I had time to reply, Auntie Mary gave one of her derisive snorts, looked at him seethingly and the result was shattering. He said not one word, and left sheepishly without protest.

But it was Mr Puw's car that followed the hearse, with Auntie Mary sitting next to her father, and Sara, Mari and myself occupying the back seat. I was ordered to wear my 'Jim Crow'. I obeyed. It wasn't the time nor the place for argument.

It was a miserable journey in the rain. We had to shelter under our umbrellas, and we travelled at the horse's pace for a distance of six miles or more. No one spoke. Never in my life had I attended a church service, never had I been inside a church. I had no idea what to expect.

At long last we arrived. I clung tightly to Auntie Mary. The Rector was waiting for us at the church gate, looking like a phantom, dressed in white. John Saer, Uncle Jim, Dyta and Mr Puw carried the coffin shoulder high, when two others joined them – Dr Powell was one, the other was an elderly man with a white beard. But he was crying and shaking intensely; so much so, that another man stepped forward to take his place.

The church was full, everybody in funeral black, and the women wore large fashionable hats. Marged appeared from nowhere, and I walked into the church holding on tightly to both Auntie Mary and Marged. The Rector was chanting all the way into the church, whilst I was trying my best to catch his words, so that I could find out the truth about the spirit. I clearly heard him say, 'When our bodies lie in the dust, our souls may live with Thee, with the Father and the Holy Spirit, world without end.'

Marged and Auntie Mary and I sat in the front pew. They both wept, whilst I was trying to be brave, refusing to shed tears, and doing my best to understand the Rector's words; but he spoke so quickly that I couldn't follow all that he said.

'We have gathered together to commend our sister Myfanwy unto the hands of the Almighty. God gave us his only begotton Son, and has delivered us from our enemy by His glorious resurrection.'

The more I heard, the more confused I became, so instead of listening, I decided to look around and gaze at the beauty of the church. By now, it had stopped raining, the sun shone, and the sunlight was pouring in through the window behind the altar. It was beautiful, but I didn't like the picture in the window. It was Christ on the cross, wearing his crown of thorns, with the blood oozing from his forehead. There was another stained glass window on the other side; the picture was not unlike that in Mari's big Bible. Christ had discarded his crown. He now had wings and was getting ready to ascend to heaven. I was amazed at all the beauty around me; never before had I seen such loveliness. I was suddenly roused by the priest's voice.

'The grace of Jesus Christ, the love of God and the fellowship of the Holy Ghost, be with us all for evermore.'

The mystery increased. The 'spirit' had now developed into a 'ghost'. The whole performance alarmed me – there were three other priests present apart from the Rector. Why? And who were all these people present? Did they know Mamo? And who was that tall gentleman with the white beard who cried all the time?

Everybody stood to sing a Welsh hymn – everybody except the mourners – myself,

Auntie Mary, Marged, Dyta, his brother, and two or three others including the bearded man.

'O fryniau Caersalem ceir gweled

Holl daith yr anialwch i gyd.'

I could not understand the meaning of the hymn either. What was the connection between the hills of Jerusalem and the people in this place? After the hymn-singing we followed the priests into the graveyard – the Rector muttering some words that I could barely hear, let alone understand.

They lowered the coffin into the deep hole, and I could see in my mind's eye, not the earth and the casket, but Mamo lying inside it, her beautiful black hair now framing her face, and wearing a brilliant blue silk gown.

'In the midst of life we are in death – deliver us from the bitterness of eternal death.'

On, and on, and on, until I could hold the tears back no longer. I felt sick too, and I had lost my handkerchief.

'Let us commend our sister into the hands of God, and commit her body to the ground, earth to earth, ashes to ashes, dust to dust.'

I felt like retching. Auntie Mary gave me her handkerchief.

'Blessed are the dead who die in the Lord so says the spirit.'

I was hanging on to Auntie Mary, and

feeling so ashamed of myself. I had made such an effort to be brave. But I had failed, and what was far worse, I had failed Mamo. I was just hoping that Dr Powell would not have noticed my tears.

The Rector carried on praying. 'Our Father which art in heaven . . .' It was such a long tedious prayer.

Then he gently took hold of my hand and led me to the graveside, to bid Mamo the final farewell. I refused to look down at the coffin, freed myself from the Rector's hand, and ran away. Auntie Mary ran after me, and caught up with me.

'Auntie Mary, I want to go home.'

'Just wait for a few minutes, darling. All these people have gathered to offer you their sympathy. There is also food laid on for us in the vestry.'

'I don't want food.'

Dr Powell arrived. 'Are you all right Jini, dear? Come with me to the vestry for a drink of water.'

I obeyed. But that was a mistake. I should have gone home, instead of loitering around, because before I had quite finished drinking the water, a crowd had gathered around me. They shook hands and uttered the most ridiculous words – words that gave me no comfort.

'God bless you, my child.'

'I'm sorry, my dear,' exactly as if they had been responsible.

'Take comfort, my dear Miss John.'

'God looks after his own.'

I had no idea who they were. Some greeted me as 'Jini', others as 'Jane', and a few even as 'Miss John'.

I liked the sound of 'Miss John'. It was proof that I was no longer a child.

The man of the white beard put his arm over my shoulder, and said in a shaky voice, 'Jane dear, don't worry, I am here to take care of you.'

Who was he? And what right did he have to take care of me?

My stomach turned at all this sympathy and soft soap, and I yearned to escape. Dyta was in his element. He enjoyed the handshakes and the sympathy, and the white handkerchief with the black edging was very much in evidence. But I kept my distance, I didn't want to be associated with him. There was a great deal of gossip and guesswork going on too.

More than once I heard whispers, 'What will become of the little girl?'

If they only knew, I had no idea myself. I overheard one fat woman with her mouth full of bread-and-butter and cheese whispering aloud to another fat woman, 'Poor little girl, she's the image of her mother. Let's hope that she will behave herself better than she did, and avoid being trampled underfoot by a scamp like Ifan.'

When the other woman realised that I was within hearing, she gave the other woman a mighty thump, with the result that she spilled her tea all over herself.

It was like the May fair in the vestry – talking, laughing, stuffing food down their throats, endless shaking of hands, whilst I was dying to go home. I had a sharp pain in my tummy, and I felt sick – sick inside me, sick of everybody, and above all, sick of myself. I was really fed up, and eager to escape from the gossip, the noise and the jollifications in the vestry. How could they?

But Dyta seemed to be enjoying himself immensely, squaring his shoulders, and joking amidst a crowd of men very much like himself. But if someone came on to sympathise he would lower his head reverently and produce the white handkerchief with the black edging.

And the tea party? Whose idea was that? Marged, I am certain had a lot to do with it. It was she who urged everybody to eat, 'Come on, eat up, there's plenty for everybody.' She was assisted by three or four girls in white lace aprons. Very smart and very correct.

Amidst all the hubbub, Dyta approached me. He was anxious to show the people present that he was concerned about me.

'Jini *fach*,' he said, 'I will be returning to Llety'r Wennol in my car,' (*my* car, if you please). 'I think you had better come with me, then Mary can go back straight to Pen-gwern.'

No,' said I without even thanking him, 'I shall be safer with Auntie Mary.'

But I so wished to go home, but I couldn't get Auntie Mary away from the white bearded man.

There they were in the corner, talking in whispers, and now and again Marged would join them, leaving me at the mercy of strangers. Sara and Mari were busily engaged with the washing up of the crockery.

At long last, Mr Puw lost his patience completely. 'Jini and I are going home – if you want a lift, Mary, you must come at once, this minute.'

She obeyed instantly.

Sara and Mari remained behind to help Marged and the maids to clear up. Obviously, they enjoyed themselves, chatting and gossiping with friends, whom they hadn't seen for a long, long time. Apparently a funeral is a real get-together.

Auntie Mary sat in front, alongside her father, whilst I sat like a lady in the back seat. The pain in my tummy persisted, and I felt as if there was a stone stuck in my stomach. Auntie Mary and her father talked non-stop in whispers, but I was able to catch a few words now and again.

'No, Mary, she is not coming to Pen-gwern, and that's final.'

They were talking about me, of course. But by now I had made my own plans. I was determined to stay at Llety'r Wennol. I would have Sara and Mari as neighbours, Dyta would be away in Pembrokeshire, and I would be careful to bolt the bedroom door, whenever he would be around.

I was disappointed in Auntie Mary too, because I heard her telling Mamo on oath that she would always look after me.

To my surprise, Dyta was waiting for us at Llety'r Wennol. Uncle Jim had returned on his own, in the car. And lo and behold, there was Dyta waiting for us, kettle on the boil, tea on the table, and ready to entertain us.

'Why didn't you accompany your brother?' asked Auntie Mary.

'I thought I would stay tonight, to keep Jini company.'

Auntie Mary glared at him long and disgustedly, and the silence that followed was far more eloquent than words.

At last Auntie Mary spoke. 'Jini is coming with me. I promised Myfi to take care of her – she didn't trust everybody.'

The car horn hooted. Mr Puw was getting impatient, and I felt that Dyta got off lightly, because of that.

'Come Jini, we must go. Ifan, may I give you a word of advice? It would be wiser if you were to leave too, because from today onwards, Llety'r Wennol will *not* be your home, that is certain.'

We left, heads held high, without further explanation, and without a word of farewell.

26

Mr Puw was an impatient man and could be gruff at times.

'Jabber, jabber! Hurry up, I want to be home in time for the news. I want to know what has become of those pig-headed miners in Carmarthenshire. They are slowly destroying our country. There wasn't a scrap of coal at Henllan station yesterday. If we don't get the better of the scoundrels, we shall all freeze to death.'

He uttered his speech in a loud voice, so that all could hear; this annoyed Auntie Mary.

'Dada, as yet it is only mid-summer. And anyway, we have enough timber in our wood to keep the home fires burning for many years.'

Mr Puw was ruffled by Auntie Mary's interference and she had to be told off in no uncertain terms.

'Shut up, Mary, you understand nothing about politics. Those colliers are greedy, grabbing men, and it is possible that we shall see another great war because of their greediness.'

Auntie Mary very wisely obeyed, and shut up.

Mr Puw had recently bought a wireless set for the first time, and that 'wireless' controlled his life. He had suddenly become an authority on law and order, and on how the country should be run. His arch-enemy was a man called Cook, a man whom he had never heard of, until he had bought his 'wireless'.

So off we went in a terrific hurry – the car bumping and thumping, and Auntie Mary and myself holding on like grim death to car straps.

'Take care Dada, you are not Malcolm Campbell and this narrow lane is not Pendine Sands.'

'Shut up, Mary.'

He took no heed; luckily we did arrive home safely, but shaken and upset.

I felt really sick at the end of that horrendous journey; my head was beating like a drum, the tummy ache was much worse. So was the *hiraeth*. I was a child of no fixed abode.

'Auntie Mary, I know it is early in the day, but I would like to go to bed.'

'Of course, Jini dear, you've had a dreadful day, but you must have a bite before you retire.'

So after a cup of tea, egg on toast, and two aspirins, I went straight to bed. I was glad to be alone. I wanted to think and plan – plan my own future. Above all else, I was determined one way or another to go to the County School. That was a solemn promise, and I couldn't let Mamo down. But how? Who would supply me with the money to buy books, clothes, and pay for my lodgings? I would have to return to Llety'r Wennol the following day to go through Mamo's jewels – maybe I would have to sell them. I would be sorry to have to do that. But education is far more important and of greater value than jewels.

If Auntie Mary had intended me to live at Pen-gwern, she should have asked me before now. And what did she mean by telling Dyta that Llety'r Wennol would not be his home for much longer? I would be quite prepared to live at Llety'r Wennol on my own, but never, never, under the same roof as Dyta. And who was that tall, white-haired, bearded man, who said that he would take care of me? Who on earth was he?

I turned and tossed, I thought and I planned. But I could not see a spark of light at the end of the dark tunnel.

At long last I slept – the pills had done their work.

When I awoke, the pain had gone, but to my sorrow and disgust, the bottom sheet was badly stained with blood. I wasn't frightened. I knew instinctively what had happened. Mamo had warned me sometime before she died that my body would change, that I would develop into womanhood, leaving childhood behind me. She said the bleeding would occur every month, and she called it 'woman's curse'. I remembered every word. She also warned me against the sins of the flesh – how I would have to guard my virginity, and on no account allow any unprincipled man or boy to take advantage of me. It was a long sermon; she spoke under great stress, and warned me against evil men who took advantage of young girls. I then asked her in all innocence, 'Did Dyta take advantage of me?'

'What your father did to you was beastly and sinful. He is a wicked man. Never, never, trust him – always keep your distance from him.'

Before I could ask any more questions, she turned her face towards the wall and cried – cried piteously for a long, long time. Never again did I have a chance to ask her more questions about the facts of life. She was dead within the month. I wept when I thought about it, and also I was so ashamed that I had messed up Auntie Mary's sheet.

I was still weeping when she brought me a cup of tea.

'Auntie Mary, I am suffering from the woman's curse.'

Before I had time to apologise, she was hugging and kissing me.

'Is this the first time?'

'Yes, Mamo had warned me about it. But it came on suddenly. I am sorry Auntie Mary.'

'Don't worry, darling. I shall see to everything. The strain of the last days has been too much for you. Come on, forget about it – get dressed, we have a busy day in front of us.'

After getting up I felt much better and felt ready to face the world's trials once more. I felt older and more mature than I did yesterday. I was no longer a child; I was now entering the revered state of womanhood.

'Auntie Mary, I would like to visit Llety'r Wennol today. I want to see my mother's jewels. They are mine now, and I want to care for them.'

'Of course, Jini. We shall do that in the morning. There is another visit to pay in the afternoon.'

Auntie Mary borrowed her father's car and away we went. I was determined to discuss my future with her today. Where would I go from here? I would be quite happy to live at Llety'r Wennol, if only Dyta would stay away. But how would I survive, without money? And apart from that, I was afraid – afraid of Dyta. How could I be certain he would stay away? He could abuse me again; he was such a strong man. I remembered Mamo's words 'never trust your father'. I had decided to discuss my future with Auntie Mary, and that sometime today. We were both silent in the car – Auntie Mary concentrating on her driving, whilst I worried about tomorrow, and every tomorrow that followed that.

When we arrived at Llety'r Wennol, we were surprised to see John Saer's bike leaning against the wall, and inside the house he was busily changing the locks.

'Who asked you to do this John? Ifan?'

'No, Miss Puw – Mr Lloyd-Williams.'

'And what about me?' I asked peevishly, 'does it mean that I cannot live here after today?'

'Oh, no, Miss John – Mr Lloyd-Williams said I was to give you a spare key, but to nobody else.'

I felt very annoyed. Who was this Lloyd-Williams? What right had he to interfere? Llety'r Wennol was and is my home.

'Miss Puw will explain to you,' he said uncomfortably, and carried on with his knocking, making far more noise than was necessary.

'Auntie Mary, who is Lloyd-Williams? And what business is it of his to change the locks?'

Auntie Mary became quite flustered, she hesitated, she coughed, and said, 'Mr Lloyd-Williams is your grandfather, Jini, and he owns Llety'r Wennol.'

The truth dawned upon me like a flash.

Of course. I remembered seeing Mamo's name in the Bible – Myfanwy Lloyd-Williams. He was the bearded man weeping at the funeral. The man who said that he would look after me. Why had I been so *twp*, so dense.

'I had arranged to tell you today, Jini. I am sorry you had to learn the truth so abruptly.'

'Never mind,' I said.

But I *did* mind. Why hadn't someone told me long ago? Why hadn't Mamo told me, or Marged? Or even Dyta? Why the secrecy? What did they have to hide? Was it my grandfather whom Marged and Mamo referred to as HE. I would have to get to the bottom of all this.

John's hammering was like an echo resounding in my head – the echo of the truth. The truth that could change my life completely.

'I will look after you, Jane'. I could see sense in those words now.

John was about to complete his mission. 'John, please leave the bolt on the bedroom door.'

'Somebody has already removed it, Miss. It wasn't me.'

A cold sweat ran over me.

'John, put it back at once.'

Auntie Mary and John looked at each other, puzzled.

'You won't need the bolt, Jini – you won't be living here.'

'Where will I live, if not at Llety'r Wennol? No one else has offered me a home.'

'Jini, listen,' she said with emphasis, 'you

will *not* be without a home. I promise you. Your grandfather changed the locks because he does not want your father to live here.'

'But John has been told to give me a spare key and therefore I want the bolt put back – in case . . .'

'In case of what, Jini?'

'In case someone breaks in whilst I'm in bed.'

'But you won't be living here, Jini.'

'Where will I live then? This is the only home I have.'

It was obvious that Auntie Mary was uncomfortable and wanted to see the back of John Saer.

John Saer was uncomfortable too, and to smooth matters he said, 'I'll come back tomorrow to fix the bolt, Miss John,' and as an after-thought he said, 'but I shall need to have a word with Mr Lloyd-Williams first.' He collected his tools, and away he went, glad to be rid of us.

I felt very satisfied with myself. I felt that I was growing up, leaving childhood behind me, and that I was able to stand my ground against both Auntie Mary and John Saer.

Auntie Mary seemed sad and defeated. It wasn't her fault that they had withheld all information from me. Everybody, even Sara and Mari had conspired to keep me in the dark. But I had grown up and matured during the last months – grief and responsibility compels one to do that, and I made up my mind that no one was going to treat me as a silly little child ever again. Furthermore, I decided to sell Mamo's treasures. I had to be independent, not to depend on charity and treated like an orphan – 'Pity, poor child'. Reading Charles Dickens had given me an insight into the plight of orphans.

'Come, Jini fach, we have no time to lose. Marged is preparing a meal for us. Today Jini, you shall meet your grandfather.'

I wasn't anxious to meet him, but maybe he would allow me to stay on at Llety'r Wennol.

But firstly I had to get hold of the jewels – they were my lifeline. I knew that the key was kept in a tin box under the bed. I found it easily, opened the lid, elated and hopeful.

But oh, the shock! Most of them had gone. The silver and velvet-lined boxes had vanished. The drawer had been full a few weeks ago.

I stood stunned and bewildered, gazing into the nearly-empty drawer. I had not only lost my fortune, but also my only chance to become independent and to get on in the world. A thief had stolen Mamo's treasures. My dream was in ruins – without their help I could never be independent.

Auntie Mary had grown pale from the shock and was speechless. When she recovered, she said, 'This is robbery, the police must be informed.'

'What's the use, Auntie Mary?'

'The jewellery was worth a great deal of money – Myfi had guarded them over the years, had sold nothing, in case she should be forced to sell them one day to pay for a real need.'

We wept once again – weeping came easily to both of us during those days of darkness.

We collected what was left in the drawer; one watch, one gold chain, one bracelet and two brooches. Five items only, where there was a hundred and more.

'Have you any idea who stole them, Jini?'

'Yes, have you?'

No names were mentioned, our thoughts ran on the same lines.

'When did it happen, Jini? Have you any idea?'

'After Mamo died, I am certain.'

'Ifan was here on his own, night after night.'

'You've named him, Auntie Mary.'

'We must go and tell your grandfather at once.'

'Why Auntie Mary, what can he do?'

'You would be surprised. He knows Ifan better than anyone. Why do you think he changed the locks?'

'I don't know – it is all a mystery to me.'

'Yes darling, I am sorry. All that happened yesterday and today too, have been a great strain on you.'

'It has been a nightmare, Auntie Mary, and I only hope that I shall wake up presently to find that it was all a bad dream.'

'We must hurry to Nant-y-wern. Tell your grandfather everything and let him act.'

I remembered, through clouds of guesswork and uncertainty, that both Dyta and his brother wore brand new suits for the funeral. They had hired a car and Dyta had bought a massive glass wreath to place on the grave. Where did the money come from? It was no good guessing, and I suddenly remembered that I too had new clothes. Who paid for those? I didn't. I would have to solve all these mysteries sooner or later. 'Let the day's woes look after themselves' – that was Mari's maxim in every crisis.

Away we went, on exactly the same route as we had followed the previous day. We came to St Michael's Church for the second time during my lifetime. It was only yesterday that I was here burying Mamo but it seemed a long, long time ago. Yesterday I was a child, today a woman.

'Would you like to see your mother's grave, Jini?'

'Yes, please.'

It did not appear so cold and earthy today; flowers adorned it. Three floral wreaths and a huge glass wreath 'In memory of my dear wife, from Ifan'. Mine was made up of white roses (who paid?), Auntie Mary's wreath was of red roses and there was another large wreath 'From all at Nant-y-wern'.

Hiraeth, tears and more tears.

'Don't cry, Jini my dear, there is sunshine behind every dark cloud.'

Words without any sort of sense or comfort.

I noticed a huge black marble headstone next to my mother's grave.

In loving memory
of
Jane Elizabeth
Beloved wife of
David Lloyd-Williams
Nant-y-wern
of this parish
Died June 1st 1896
Aged 26 years.
'Many women have done virtuously,
But thou excellest them all.'

'Your grandmother's grave, Jini.'

'How strange, June 1st, Mamo's birthday.'

'Your grandmother died giving birth to your mother.'

I stood in silence – not in surprise, but out of respect, as we do during the two minutes' silence on Armistice Day.

'Where is my little brother buried?'

'In the same grave as your mother.'

I felt glad that my Grandmother, little David and Mamo, lay alongside in the same place, in the same earth in St Michael's Church. They would be company for one another.'

'Auntie Mary, do you believe in the resurrection?'

'Yes.'

'Have you proof?'

'That was how I was taught.'

'But that's no proof.'

'Perhaps not, but if the bishops and the priests believe in the resurrection, who am I to doubt their faith.'

No, I couldn't argue with her over that. It is better neither to doubt nor argue where religion is concerned. So religion was dropped.

We drove on in silence. I felt nervous and uncertain. We arrived at a large wrought-iron gate. Auntie Mary went out of the car to open it. We then drove up a narrow road which she called 'the drive', and saw rising in front of us a big stately house of grey stone, and on the lawn in front of the house strutted two proud peacocks.

We had arrived at Nant-y-wern, Dad-cu's home, and the house where Mamo was brought up as a child.

27

Shock! Shock after shock after shock! My small world was shattered. Here was Mamo's home as a young girl, and to crown it all Auntie Mary declared in a flat 'I-know-everything' voice, 'All this will be yours one day, provided you behave yourself and please your grandfather.'

That made me nervous and unsure of myself, exactly as if I was taking part in a romantic fairy tale, happy-ever-after, kind of drama. But some of the magic disappeared when I saw Marged, arms akimbo, standing solidly on the doorstep. 'Welcome girls. Welcome to Nant-y-wern.'

I had no time to loiter and look around, but what struck me at first glance was the shine and polish everywhere. Even the floor sparkled. We had earthenware tiles at Llety'r Wennol.

'Take off your coats, make yourself at home – food is ready.'

Just plain, ordinary words, in an extraordinary situation. Marged, always practical, with her feet set solidly on the ground. Marged who had been faithful to Mamo throughout the years in spite of all the difficulties – in spite of her poverty and sin. And she must have sinned unforgiveably, otherwise why did she have to live in hardship and shame, whilst her father lived in luxury in a big house?

Sitting at the top of the table was the bearded man who wept at Mamo's funeral – Dad-cu, my grandfather. He did not stand to receive us, and I had the feeling that he too was rather nervous.

'Hullo!' he said, without even glancing at us. 'Sit down.'

Marged did all the talking. She chattered non-stop about the most trivial things – the weather, the wind blowing down the smoke in the kitchen, how Maggie the maid had forgotten to close the back door, allowing the dog to escape. On and on without a break. Chattering to drown the silence.

I looked around in amazement – everything shone in this room too, from the fine china to the silver on the table. I had never seen such a beautifully-laid table, and a young girl, complete with lace cap and apron attended to our needs. Real style! But for Marged's tittle-tattle it would have been a meal in silence. Seeing all this grandeur around us, I could not help thinking of Mamo. She left all this to live like a pauper, eating from cracked plates and cooking the simplest of food on an open fire.

Dad-cu at last broke the silence, and said again, without looking up, 'You were late arriving,' partly a question and partly a reprimand.

'Yes, we called to see the flowers in the graveyard.'

As usual Marged had to say something; it would have been wiser if she had shut up.

'There was a most beautiful wreath from Ifan. Fair play to him.'

Dad-cu got up like a bullet, thumped the table until the china rattled, and yelled in an angry voice, 'I don't want that scoundrel's name ever mentioned in this house again. Do you hear me? Never again.' And he stalked out.

Marged was not at all perturbed; she merely said, 'Poor Mr Lloyd-Williams, he has been so upset of late – the funeral yesterday has left its mark on him.'

In order to change the subject, she turned to Auntie Mary and asked her straight out, 'Have you fixed the date of your big day, Mary?'

Auntie Mary changed colour; suddenly her face was a purplish red, and she lowered her head as if in prayer.

Another major shock – 'big day' could only mean one thing. Auntie Mary was planning to get married!

'Haven't you told Jane about your wedding, Mary?'

Auntie Mary did not lift her head. She blew her nose loudly and said in a subdued apologetic voice, 'I haven't had a chance to tell her, because Myfi was so very ill, and for such a long time.'

I pouted and had a job to stop myself from crying. After all, I depended on Auntie Mary. She was the person who was going to take the place of Mamo in my life. She was also supposed to be my guardian, and it was she who assured me that I would never be homeless. And now she was planning to get married without even telling me. Why?

Disappointment! Shock! Auntie Mary noticed my distress and lifted her head to recite the same old adage, which I was really fed up of hearing.

'Don't worry, Jini. I will take care of you. I will make certain that you will never be homeless.'

'What does that mean, Auntie Mary? Does it mean that I can live with you after you are married.'

Marged, as the person who knew it all, spoke with authority. 'You can't possibly do that, Jane. Mary is going to Swansea to live.'

Another rebuff.

'Listen Jini, darling.' I was listening. 'I am truly sorry. I meant to tell you everything today, and also ask you to act as my bridesmaid. Will you, Jini? Please?'

I didn't reply. I wanted time to arrange my confused thoughts, time to consider my future. I got up in a huff and out I went by way of the massive front door, out to the peacocks. As I approached, the larger of the two gave an unearthly screech, which echoed my disturbed thoughts – a long, sad screech like a voice from another world. He spread his colourful tail and the gorgeous hues reminded me of the stained glass windows in the church the day of Mamo's funeral. That was only yesterday – but it seemed a long, long time ago. And here was I – an orphan and homeless. Admittedly, I had a father, but a father who was a responsibility and a disgrace. I preferred to be fatherless.

'I don't want to hear that scoundrel's name ever again in this house' were Dad-cu's words, and he was right.

There was a long bench on the lawn. I sat on it, in order to gaze at the peacocks and think. I arrived at a decision, the turning point in my life. Who should come but my grandfather – my one chance had arrived; and he appeared to have forgotten his bout of indignation.

'Do you fancy the peacocks, Jane?'

'Yes, Sir – they are beautiful.'

'Jane, pay attention to me. I am not 'Sir' to you. I am your grandfather, so call me by my proper name – Dad-cu.'

'Yes, Dad-cu, thank you,' and the name slipped out easily. I was happy with it.

I took advantage of the chance.

'Dad-cu, I want to ask you a favour.'

'Yes, what is it?'

'Would you kindly allow me to live at Llety'r Wennol – that is, on my own?'

'No, definitely not. I will not allow that.'

'But what shall I do? Auntie Mary is getting married, and I have nowhere else to live.'

Silence, dead silence – even the peacocks were quiet. After minutes of embarassment he said slowly and gently, 'Would you like to come and live here with Marged and me?'

'But I must attend the County School; I promised Mamo on her death-bed that I would do so, in order to get on in the world.'

I had recited those words so many times to myself and to others with the result that they sounded like an ancient proverb.

'You shall certainly be allowed to attend the County School or a Residential School if you so wish.'

'No – it's the County School I want.'

'That's settled then. But there is one condition which I insist that you keep – at all times.'

'Yes, Dadcu?' I rather liked the sound of that word.

'You must break all connections with your father. You must never again have anything to do with him. Understand?'

'Yes, perfectly, Dad-cu. I have no wish to see him ever again.'

'You too have recognised him for what he really is. It is a pity your mother didn't.'

Dad-cu's offer pleased me, but I had not promised to accept it. My mind was more at ease, but I was still confused and undecided, and I had no one in whom I could confide. Even Auntie Mary had failed me.

'Come, Jane. Marged will show you over the house.'

In we went.

We began our journey in the dining room, with its sumptuous furniture and its silver, down through a long passage to the main kitchen, the back kitchen and the dairy. I was introduced to the two maids, Lizzie and Maggie.

'Meet Miss Jane,' said Marged.

They both curtsied and said, 'Pleased to meet you, Miss Jane.'

'No,' said I, 'not *Miss* Jane, please. Just Jane without the Miss.'

Marged frowned.

I didn't fancy such high and mighty ways – but I preferred Jane to Jini.

The kitchen was huge, shining like the rest of the house, and you could have easily fitted Llety'r Wennol right inside it.

I followed her up the wide oak staircase to half a dozen bedrooms with a four-poster in each, apart from one. That was completely empty with the curtains drawn.

'This was your mother's bedroom.'

'Why is it unfurnished?'

'The furniture is in the bedroom at Llety'r Wennol.'

Of course, that explained why the bedroom furniture was so superior and of a different class from all the other bits and pieces in the house.

We came down stairs – I had seen enough. I was overpowered with a wave of *hiraeth* and of pity. To think that Mamo had to struggle against poverty through all those years, whilst her father lived in the lap of luxury. I was convinced that somehow or other it was Dyta's fault. But why? Why? I was angry too, and determined to get to the truth and solve the mystery. There were other rooms to inspect, the wash-rooms and the servants' quarters, but I had lost all interest. I longed for Llety'r Wennol and the simple way of life. I was happy there – when Dyta wasn't around.

We entered the parlour – furnished with beautiful pictures, with red velvet settees and chairs. There we found Dad-cu and Auntie Mary talking in whispers and it was obvious that both had been shedding tears – tears of regret, hopefully.

I was dumbfounded. I could not utter a word. My tongue was bone-dry and my head was reeling. I had worried in the past about being left homeless, and here I was being offered a home in a grand old house with two peacocks into the bargain, and I didn't have the grace to accept it.

I was uncertain of myself and of Dad-cu too. After all, he turned out his only daughter from her rightful home and allowed her to wither away in the company of Dyta in a lowly cottage. Why? Maybe if I came to this house to live, I would one day have to suffer the same treatment. And yet he appeared to be a kindly old man, although he had lost his temper very quickly during dinner time. Nobody is perfect.

'Don't you like this place, Jini? Would you not be happy to live here with me?'

Before I had a chance to reply, Auntie Mary intervened. I could see that she was afraid I would turn down the offer.

'I have told Mr Lloyd-Williams about the theft of the jewellery and that we suspect your father.'

'I don't think Ifan would stoop to that – Ifan wasn't a thief,' said Marged, who saw some goodness in every blackguard.

'Shut up, for goodness' sake,' said Dad-cu sharply. 'Go and prepare tea for us.'

She obeyed quietly; it was obvious who was the boss.

Dad-cu then turned to me and addressed me solemnly like a judge. 'Jane, I want you to tell me everything. I want the truth, the whole truth, so think carefully before you reply. Take your time.'

He coughed, a cough of authority, and started on his questioning, 'When did you last see the jewels, Jane?'

'A month or so before my mother died.'

'What did your mother tell you?'

'These one day will be yours – look after them carefully.'

'Did your father know about them?'

'I suppose so. I'm not certain.'

'Where was the key kept?'

'In a tin box under the bed.'

'Did your father stay in the house at any time on his own?'

'Yes, he was on night-watch on his own for three nights.'

And so it went on and on, until I felt that I was partly responsible for the theft. I showed what was left – they were still in my pocket.

'Here they are, Dad-cu – one chain, one watch, one bracelet, and two brooches.'

He took hold of the big brooch with the blue stone and gazed at it lovingly.

'The thief didn't know much about the value of jewellery, or he would have taken this. It is the brooch that I bought for your grandmother whilst we were on our honeymoon. It is very valuable, treasure it.'

His voice cracked and his eyes became misty. I just couldn't answer him – my voice was cracking too. But he soon composed himself and said with confidence, 'If they have only recently been stolen, there is hope that we will be able to trace most of them. I shall see my solicitor first thing tomorrow morning. Leave it all to me.'

Dad-cu obviously was a man of action.

Auntie Mary was snuffling into her handkerchief, Dad-cu joined in and said under great stress, 'Myfanwy, poor dear. God only knows what she had to suffer, but never once did she complain – neither did she beg for charity.'

The silence that followed was deadly, and it spoke volumes. I felt awkward and conscious of my new position in life as a woman and a grown-up person. I stood up, full of my new importance in life, and said clearly and emphatically. 'I want to say something, Dad-cu. I would be very pleased if I could come here to live with you.'

Dad-cu did not reply, but he got up and was on the point of embracing me. But I moved away quickly and managed to avoid him. I could not suffer any man to touch me – in my experience, embracing and pawing always ended in abuse and torture.

26

There never was such a day – a day of disclosing secrets, a day of surprises, and a day of shocks and disappointments. I should have revelled in my luxurious new-found home, but I yearned to return to Llety'r Wennol, to tranquility and the simple life. As Mari used to say, 'a chick brought up in the warmth of hell will want to remain there all the days of its life'.

But I had to accompany Auntie Mary back to Pen-gwern. 'You shall *not* stay at Llety'r Wennol on your own, your grandfather would never forgive me if I allowed you to do that.'

'My grandfather is not my custodian.'

'Where did you learn that word, Jini? You are very knowledgeable.'

'You have to be or you'll never be able to enter college as I intend to do.'

'Well, at your age, I'm afraid you will have to have a custodian. It's up to you to choose between your father and grandfather.'

I didn't answer her. I still felt annoyed, and sour towards her. She should have told me about her marriage. It was mean of her to allow Marged to let the cat out of the bag. But if I had to choose between Dad-cu and Dyta as my custodian, I would have definitely preferred

Dad-cu. I didn't want to have anything to do with Dyta ever again.

Auntie Mary was quiet and subdued all the way back to Pen-gwern. She was welcome to pout, if that was how she wished to behave.

When we arrived she merely said, 'We had better retire early. We have a busy week in front of us. We must go shopping for your school outfit, also clothes for the wedding. You *are* prepared to act as bridesmaid, Jini?'

I didn't reply; the hurt still remained deep down inside.

'Please, Jini.'

'I suppose so,' I answered half-heartedly.

'Thank you, darling. I am so sorry that you had to learn about it in such a casual way. I should have told you myself. I was at fault.'

'Yes you were, Auntie Mary.'

The pain still gnawed, and I went upstairs without even bidding her goodnight. Nor did I thank her, but cried myself to sleep.

The following day, away we went to buy new clothes. Last week we went shopping for mourning clothes. Today we were on our way to buy bridal clothes.

'Who pays for my new clothes, Auntie Mary?'

'Don't worry about paying. Enjoy yourself.'

'Who, Auntie Mary? I must know.'

'They will be paid for. Don't distress yourself.'

'Who, Auntie Mary?'

'You are as stubborn as a mule.'

'Yes I am. Once more – who? I must know, or . . .'

'Your grandfather, but he asked me not to tell you.'

'Did you ask him for the money?'

'No Jini, he was anxious to pay for everything. He has more than enough. He won't miss the little he gives you.'

'That's not the point, Auntie Mary. I shall pay it back one day.'

'Don't distress yourself, child. After all, that money is only a tiny part, a very tiny part of your inheritance.'

I still didn't understand, but I sensed that Auntie Mary was fed up with my questions and my ingratitude. Nobody, not even Auntie Mary, had realised that I was a child no longer, and that I was on the threshold of developing into a mature woman.

We bought, we spent – money was no object. School clothes first, and it struck me forcibly that but for Dad-cu's generosity, I would never have been able to equip myself adequately for school. Part of my inheritance? Did I have a right to this money? The whole situation was beyond my understanding.

By the end of the day I felt like Cinderella, especially when I dressed myself in the bridesmaid array. It was a full-length pink dress with a pink bonnet to match, and white shoes and gloves. It wasn't Jini's reflection that I saw in the mirror. Miss Jane maybe – but certainly not Jini! But the prince was missing. Dad-cu with his white beard could not possibly have acted the part – he could portray Santa Claus perhaps, but never the dashing Prince Charming.

'You look like a princess, Jini. I have never seen anyone looking so dignified and beautiful.'

The tears started to roll – they came easily to us both.

'I wish your mother could see you now.'

'Yes, Auntie Mary, so do I.'

We arrived home laden with parcels to find Mr Puw in a bad mood – the rain had spoilt the hay, the sheep had developed maggots, and he was starving. So Auntie Mary, although she was dead tired, had to rush around to prepare supper for him and the farm labourers. Who would cook his meals after she was married? I put the question to her after supper.

'That worries me, Jini. I have looked after my father and acted as his housekeeper ever since my mother died, and Alun has been very patient and understanding for many years, but matters came to a head recently, and I had to choose between my father and my fiancé. In the end your mother gave me courage to make the final decision.'

'Mamo? How strange, because her marriage

was anything but successful. What possessed her to marry Dyta, of all people.'

Auntie Mary became very quiet and subdued. At last she said in an apologetic, timid voice, 'She was forced to marry, Jini.'

'Forced? Who forced her?'

Another pause – a painful pause. I knew she would tell me more if I was patient, so I asked no further questions.

'It was the effect of the scorn of a respectable society, and a father who nearly died from the shame and disgrace. Myfi was not quite eighteen, a brilliant student, and had been offered a place in Oxford. Then came the tragedy.'

'Tragedy? What tragedy?'

'She was pregnant, and forced to marry the father of her child.'

'Pregnant? With me?'

'Yes, with you, Jini.'

'But why, Auntie Mary?'

'I don't know. It still remains a mystery. She was young, rich, and very beautiful, and Ifan enticed her. He too was a good looking fellow, with a plausible tongue, and she fell into his snare. Ifan was the head horseman at Nant-y-wern, and Myfi was a very good catch.'

'Perhaps she was manhandled and abused – then it couldn't have been her fault. He used to maltreat Mamo continuously. I used to hear her groaning and crying from my bed in the loft.'

'Jini darling, you've had to grow up at a very early age. Honestly, I don't know what actually happened. All I know is that she was turned out of her home, given Llety'r Wennol as a home, and also a sum of money. But it didn't take Ifan long to go through that.'

'Why didn't someone tell me about this? Why didn't you, Auntie Mary?'

'It was not a topic to talk about – it was taboo. The humiliation and the shame were unbearable.'

Auntie Mary wept.

'Who was John?'

'What do you know of John?'

'John called at Llety'r Wennol to bid goodbye before he was posted to France. They hugged, they kissed and they cried for a long time. They took no notice of me, but Mamo warned me not to tell a soul.'

'John was her childhood sweetheart, and was accepted by her father. He was a couple of years older than Myfi, and studied medicine in London. He was very upset indeed when she married Ifan. Poor Myfi, she paid dearly for her blunder.'

'It was more than a blunder, Auntie Mary, it was a sin, and the Bible tells us that sin must be punished.'

'Goodness me, Jini, you are well up in your Biblical knowledge. But don't you pass judgement on your mother. You are just as bad as your grandfather and the chapel deacons. They excommunicate girls who sin, in case they might defile their place of worship. Never judge, Jini, unless you are certain of your facts.'

I wasn't sorry for what I said, but in order to calm the troubled waters, I declared in a voice of I-know-best, 'But if you are abused and forced, then it is not the woman's fault.'

'Of course not, Jini.'

'Dyta is a man who takes advantage. No woman is safe when he is around.'

'Jini dear, you know far too much for your age. You have grown up far too early. Every man is not like your father.'

'I don't trust any man. I can never forget what my father and the Master did to me. All men are the same. You watch out, Auntie Mary.'

She looked at me with sorrow in her eyes and said nothing. I only hoped that she would fare better than poor Mamo did, and that no man would take advantage of her. In spite of everything, I loved Auntie Mary.

Those were hectic days – cleaning the house from top to bottom, preparing for the 'big day', and doing our best to humour Mr Puw, who walked around the place as if in a trance. The new housekeeper had arrived – a big strapping woman who moved everything and everybody who stood in her way, including Mr Puw. He, in turn, ignored her completely. All this irritated and vexed Auntie Mary; but she stood her ground. There was no turning back now.

She informed her father in no uncertain terms, 'Dada, my future is at stake. I cannot expect Alun to wait for me any longer. His business is in Swansea, therefore I have to uproot myself and move to live with him. I promise to visit you whenever possible – Swansea is only fifty miles away.'

His only answer was a grunt.

I enjoyed myself at Pen-gwern – I fed the chicks, I played with the dogs, and rode the white pony. I also learnt to mount and control Auntie Mary's bike. But in spite of the freedom and the luxury, I hankered after Llety'r Wennol. I had grown up there within its bare walls, it was there that I had experienced distress and loneliness, hatred and affection, and also many a happy spell amidst the gloom. I missed Glan-dŵr too, my refuge at all times. I even longed to see the haughty red cockerel, who reminded me of Dyta.

So, one bright morning, I borrowed Auntie Mary's bike and cycled to my old home, with the key, that John the Carpenter had given me, safe in my pocket. I called at Glan-dŵr on the way to warn them that I would need some of their cawl at midday.

But when I arrived at my destination, I was

taken aback to see Dyta's rickety old bike leaning against the wall, and there was Dyta himself swearing and rattling the door.

'Who the devil has been fucking around with the bloody lock? It won't budge.'

'It's Dad-cu,' I said quietly, although I was trembling like a reed.

'Dad-cu? Bloody saintly Dad-cu is it? Well, well, who'd have thought! Dad-cu, old Dick himself has at last forgiven Jini *fach* for being born. You watch out my gel, or he'll turn you out of your home too, just as he did to your mother. Did he give you a key?'

'No,' the lie slipped out easily. I was terrified of finding myself inside the house with Dyta. I had not forgotten the damage and the humiliation I had suffered just before Mamo died.

'What did the bloody saint tell you? Lies, lies and still more lies I s'pose?'

'Who, Dad-cu?'

'Yes, the bugger. He's the devil himself. Never, never, trust him, my gel.'

'You don't like him, do you?'

'Like him? Hell's bells, him is the greatest bloody liar on God's earth. I shall be more than glad to go t'other place. And he says that it was me who seduced and damaged his little gel, the bloody fool.'

I couldn't stand it any longer. 'If was you who brought Mamo into trouble and disgrace.'

'Me? Me, did you say? Who told you that damn lie. Believe you me, your pretty little mother wasn't a saint. She were a hot little bitch, and spent the evenings in the stable loft with us men. She got what she asked for, and it was poor me who got landed with the mess.'

Then *I* exploded. It would have been wiser if I'd held my tongue. But I was boiling over, and my hatred towards him got the better of me. 'Mamo was a fine woman, gentle and caring. She had a hell of a life with you. She was belittled, scorned – yes, and abused too. You are a cruel beast, and I haven't forgotten what you did to me either. Remember? You are a vulgar, dirty pig.'

For a second he was stunned by my flow of words. Then suddenly, without warning, he gave me a vicious swipe on the face. It was more than a swipe, it was like a boxer's punch, which sent me reeling to the ground, with blood streaming down my face. In spite of the shock and pain I managed to get hold of the bike, mount it, and shout at the same time, 'You are the very devil, Dyta, and I never want to see you again, not as long as I live.'

I pedalled furiously with all my strength, hair dishevelled, blood streaming from my nose, towards Glan-dŵr, towards comfort and sympathy. I could hear Dyta shouting after me.

'Jini, come back, sorry I am, gel, sorry, sorry. I want to be friends. Come back Jini, come back.'

Too late, too late. I would never want to be his 'friend' – ever again. Nor would I want to see him again. I had finished with him for ever.

By the time I arrived at Glan-dŵr I was really ill, and I must have been a sorry sight. My cheek was swollen, my nose was still bleeding and I was suffering from shock. My self-respect also had had a severe knock.

Sara gasped when she saw my condition. She immediately bathed my face, put a penny on the nape of my neck to stop the nose bleeding, and whispered comforting words.

'Who is responsible Jini?'

'Dyta.'

Throughout the years, I had never carried tales – never told them of our trials and tribulations. But by today I had lost all respect for my father, and I was neither going to defend nor protect him any longer. I had finished with him – for all time.

I had lost all appetite for the *cawl*, and my face was becoming more and more swollen. Mari gave me some nauseating medicine to take, and I slept soundly on their sofa all afternoon. But I had to get back to Pen-gwern. Auntie Mary would be worried. I had lost my chance to visit Llety'r Wennol.

I insisted on cycling back. I arrived tired, in great pain and sick at heart. I tried to enter the house quietly by the back door, but Auntie Mary heard, and I had to face not only her but also Mr Puw and Dad-cu. He had come over to arrange about the date of my removal to Nant-y-wern. When they saw my condition I had to tell them everything, and I was more than willing to oblige. Dad-cu then declared with authority, 'This is a matter for the police. The man is no better than a beast – only the worst type of bully would batter an innocent child like Jane.'

But I persuaded him to leave the police out of it, not only for my sake, but for Mamo's sake too. It was important for me to guard her memory. I didn't want people to gossip about our family, maybe have fun spreading rumours, and resurrecting old scandals. Once the police are informed, you never know where or how it might end, and neither did I want people to read about it in the *Tivy-side*.

Luckily, he agreed. He wanted to know when I could move to Nant-y-wern. He seemed anxious and eager, and I thought that it augured well for my future.

So the following Saturday I packed all my personal belongings in a straw basket, rode in style in Auntie Mary's car, to start life anew in a stately manor, where there were two fine peacocks parading on the lawn in front of the house.

29

Moving to Nant-y-wern was an emotional experience. I compared myself to a wild flower being uprooted from poor, untilled soil and planted in rich fertile land. The shock usually kills the plant. Being dug up so suddenly certainly gave me a nasty jolt, and to help me to settle, I felt that I had to have some of the furniture and bits and pieces from Llety'r Wennol. My belongings did not amount to much – the books under the bed, the tea-set with the gold rim, Mamo's clothes, and the few toys that belonged to my little brother. Those were mine by right.

Mamo's old bedroom remained bare and empty at Nant-y-wern, and I asked Marged (knowing full well that she would mention it to Dad-cu) whether I could move the furniture from Mamo's old bedroom, back to the empty bedroom at Nant-y-wern, and have it as my own private room. It was the finest room in the house, a spacious room, with windows over-looking the lawn and the countryside. You could even see the church steeple in the distance – the church where Mamo was buried.

Dad-cu was more than willing, so one fine morning off we went in the big *gambo* to fetch whatever I needed from Llety'r Wennol. Sara and Mari saw the 'carnival' on its way, so they too joined us, and came to help. They took whatever I didn't want. No one gave Dyta a thought. I took a peep into the loft, and saw Dyta's belongings in confusion all over the place. Sara wanted to tidy up the mess. But I suddenly realised that I was the boss, and that it was I, and I alone, who had the right to direct and command. It was a pleasant feeling, and I made the most of it. 'No, don't touch anything; let Dyta sort out his own mess.'

Hiraeth gripped me, a yearning for my childhood. I didn't have much joy as a child – very few toys, and more affection at Glan-dŵr than I had at home, but it was here, and nowhere else, that I felt safe, especially when Dyta was away. He was the stumbling block, he was the bad influence and the more I thought about him, the more I hated him. Unfortunately, hatred embitters the soul, and makes one resentful and sour. I would have to try and forget about Dyta and his coarseness, and start anew.

At the end of the day we started for Nant-y-wern like vagrant travellers, complete with the furniture, my bits and pieces, and Marged and myself sitting precariously on top of everything, with the two manservants sitting in front, enjoying themselves, smoking and shouting an occasional gee-up at the dawdling horse.

Sara and Mari bade us goodbye, waving their handkerchiefs half-heartedly – they also used them to wipe away their tears. I had to use the sleeve of my jersey. Parting was not easy. It took us nearly three hours to arrive at our destination, a distance of about seven miles.

Sleeping in Mamo's bed with the familiar furniture around me made me feel more settled and at home. Mamo's clothes filled the big wardrobe. Marged and Auntie Mary tried to persuade me to get rid of them.

No, never. I insisted on keeping them. Apart from the fact that they were beautiful and stylish, they were the link between me and the past, between me and Mamo. When *hiraeth* overcame me I would open the wardrobe door, touch the clothes reverently, and I would feel a wonderful bond with the past, a sense of kinship. They provided me with the right to live in Dad-cu's house. It is difficult to describe the sensation.

My lifestyle changed completely. Dad-cu, Marged and I ate in the small dining-room, with a maid waiting on us. Marged persisted in addressing me as Miss Jane, regardless of my wishes. She insisted on sticking to some old-fashioned code of behaviour, which she called the 'rules of etiquette'.

Dad-cu looked after me well, without any sort of fuss or bother – he paid for everything;

he found lodgings for me in town in preparation for entering the County School. He bought me a bicycle, and promised that I should have a car when I would be of age to obtain a licence. He was successful in recouping most of the jewellery, too, and he presented them to me one day.

'There are still some of them missing. Your father was responsible. But I believe it is wiser to leave well alone – I don't wish to disturb dirty waters, and see the gossip-mongers enjoying themselves. Take good care of them Jane, they are valuable.'

Another time, he gave me a stern warning. 'You are not on any account to go out to the yard, nor to the stables, nor to the fields to chat with the menservants. Do you promise? Do you promise me faithfully not to go Jane? Do you understand?'

'Yes, Dad-cu, I understand.'

I knew why, but I said nothing. It is better to remain silent on certain occasions.

I had so much to learn about Dad-cu and the way of life at Nant-y-wern. I felt like a foreigner, an outcast who did not fit in with their mode of living. I wanted to have fun with the girls in the back kitchen and I wanted to help them with their chores. They never addressed me as Miss Jane unless Marged was around. They called her Miss Powell and 'She' behind her back. Marged was always on her high horse, and very curt and ungracious towards the maids. I was amazed to see that aspect of her character. Who was she when all was said and done? Was she related to Dad-cu? Or was she just the housekeeper?

Luckily, there was plenty of reading material around. The *Western Mail* was delivered daily, the *Farmer and Stockbreeder* and the *Tivy-side* every Saturday. There were also shelves of books in the small parlour, mostly Biblical, and also the wireless – but the few Welsh programmes we had were flawed and muffled. They sounded like bacon and egg cooking in the frying pan.

There was no talk or chatter after supper, and I was not allowed to join the maids in the kitchen.

We sat around the fireplace – Dad-cu reading the newspaper, and I trying to read one of Mamo's old books. Marged as usual chattered non-stop about nothing at all, mainly to herself. I did my best not to listen – Dad-cu managed to ignore her completely. Perhaps in time I would learn to do the same.

I had lived there for over a month. I had all I wanted, everybody was kind and courteous. I'd never had it so good. And yet I felt like a fish out of water, a stranger in my own home. Life was too comfortable, too easy-going, like the calm before the storm.

And it did happen. The storm erupted

suddenly one afternoon after lunch. Marged was fussing around, clearing the table, and Dad-cu was more talkative than usual. Then suddenly, without warning, he embraced me and said with emotion, 'Jane, you are a lovely girl, you are growing up to be just like your grandmother. I only hope you will grow up to be just like her, and that you will turn out to be as good a woman as she was.' He kissed me on my forehead.

I was petrified. I shrugged myself from his grip and ran – as far away from him as I could. The bike! Luckily it was just outside the door, and off I went with Dad-cu shouting after me, 'Jane, what's the matter? Why are you running away?'

'I've suddenly remembered that Auntie Mary wants to see me about my bridesmaid's dress,' I shouted back. A downright lie of course. I had to escape from him. Was he too at the same game as Dyta and the Master? Did every girl have to suffer like me in order to develop into a fully-grown woman? That's what Dyta told me. The crushing, the kissing and the torture were all part of the training, and now Dad-cu had started on the same stunt. I was at the end of my tether. What could I do? Only Auntie Mary could help me.

I arrived at Pen-gwern out of breath and

sweating like a pig. I ran wildly into the house. Luckily she was at home.

'Jini, what's wrong? You look as if you have seen a ghost.'

'It's Dad-cu,' I gasped.

'Your grandfather? What has he done?'

'He took advantage of me. He was aiming at abusing me. The shame of it.'

'Calm down, calm down. I just can't believe that. I know him too well. Tell me exactly what happened.'

'He placed his hands over my shoulder. Told me that I was a lovely girl and he kissed me, Auntie Mary.'

'Is that all?'

'But that is how Dyta started on his antics.'

'Jini dear, your Dad-cu loves you genuinely with a true and tender love. You are a very lucky girl, Jini.'

'Lucky? I don't understand.'

'It is the difference between clean and dirty.'

'I still don't understand.'

'Listen, listen carefully. You have now taken the place of the daughter he lost, and he wants to love and cherish you, as he cherished her. Myfanwy was the light of his life, and he spoilt her hopelessly. She would throw her arms around his neck, kiss him, and wheedle anything she wanted from him. The shock he suffered when she married Ifan nearly killed him. It changed him completely. From being a happy, jolly man, he developed into a sour, cantankerous person. And now you have risen from the dust and sorrow of the past to give him comfort in his old age, and reparation for his daughter's misdeeds. Make the most of your privilege, Jini.'

'Men scare me, Auntie Mary. I can't bear any man to touch me. Even the boys at school used to throw me into a panic. Wili Weirglodd and his mates used to run after us with their "pieces" hanging out. It was ghastly.'

'Wili Weirglodd and his chums were naughty children – not old enough to realise what they were doing. They were just playing around, having fun.'

'But how am I to recognise the difference between this clean, caring love and that other dirty love.'

'Your father is an evil man. No father should ever treat his child as you were treated. That was a dirty, unholy love, and that kind of treatment deserves punishment. It is called incest, and it is a crime. It is an experience that wrecks the soul and the life of the sufferer. The Master also – he was another wicked man who took advantage of innocent children under his care. He too should have been punished and dismissed from his job.'

'I'm still confused, Auntie Mary. My head is in a turmoil.'

'Yes, of course, darling. I understand perfectly. You have been most unfortunate. Not every man is like your father and the Master. You loved your mother, Jini?'

'Of course I loved Mamo. I thought the world of her. I love you too, Auntie Mary.'

'Well that is the kind of love your grandfather feels for you. His wife – your grandmother – died giving birth to your mother, and that is when Marged arrived at Nant-y-wern. She was employed as a nanny. But she was a second mother to Myfi, and she too worshipped her. Myfi was spoilt from the cradle. She had all she wanted and more – the best possible education, then a Boarding School in the south of England. I was lucky enough to be educated in her shadow, and accompany her to that elite school in England – Mr Lloyd-Williams paying my fees as well as his daughter's. I went there for the sole purpose of keeping Myfanwy company. But when I was fifteen my mother died suddenly, and I had to return home to take my mother's place, and to look after my father. By that time, Myfi had settled down, made new friends. She was popular, a born leader and also very gifted. Myfi was a pampered child. Between her father and Marged, she was hopelessly spoilt and lacked for nothing. She was also very affectionate, very sincere and loyal to her friends. It was no wonder her father was hurt and was so unforgiving. No one knows the depths of his suffering.'

After listening to Auntie Mary I felt that I understood the situation more clearly. I also realised the extent of Mamo's suffering. The shame and the disgrace, and also having to put up with Dyta's cruelty. Poor, darling Mamo; and it would have been so much worse but for Auntie Mary's love and loyalty. Marged too – she stuck by her to the very end.

I felt that I had to ask Auntie Mary one other all-important question. 'Auntie Mary, do you love Alun as much as you love your father?'

'Yes Jini, more so, if anything.'

'How do you know?'

'Because I am prepared to leave my father to live with Alun.'

'Are you quite sure, Auntie Mary?'

'Yes, Jini. My love for Alun is different. It is thrilling and exciting. It causes the heart to beat at a faster rate. One day you will understand. But take care. Don't fall into the same pit as your mother did. Go home, Jini, and thank the good Lord that at last you have a home that is worthy of you, and that you have a grandfather who loves you dearly, and who will never, never, take advantage of you, believe you me.'

I went home wiser and easier in my mind than I was when I arrived.

During the last few weeks I had progressed from a timid, inexperienced child who had suffered cruelty and sexual torment from two evil men, to an older and wiser girl who was on the verge of maturity, and who was fast learning about human nature and its pitfalls. From now on I would have to act with wisdom and perception, to deliberate between right and wrong, and also learn to differentiate between true love and that other dirty love, which I had been so unfortunate to experience as a child. I would have to behave sensibly at all times and aim at being the mistress of my own destiny. An arduous task to fulfil.

When I arrived home, Dad-cu and Marged were waiting for me, and supper was laid on the table. Dad-cu greeted me at the door. 'I was worried, Jane. I'm so glad you have arrived back safely. Did you enjoy yourself? Did the dress fit you?'

I had forgotten the lie, and I felt ashamed. 'Yes, thank you, Dad-cu. I had a grand time, and I learnt quite a lot too.'

I took hold of his hand and I gave him a shy kiss on his cheek. I am sure I saw him blush. A serene, warm feeling, encompassed me – a feeling of contentment and belonging, and also the knowledge that at last I had found a man whom I could trust.

I retired early. I wanted to reflect on the day's events. I wanted to plan and dream about my future. I decided to change my name – Jini John – I never fancied it. It belonged to my miserable childhood, and to my father – a father whom I never wanted to see again. 'Jane Lloyd-Williams'. I liked the sound of that. It suited my new lifestyle too, and it was a name which was more in keeping with the lawn and the peacocks.

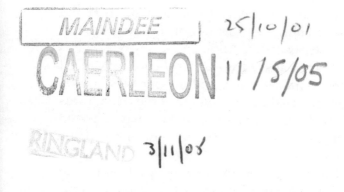